Copycat

Also by Kimberla Lawson Roby

Copycat

KIMBERLA LAWSON ROBY

GRAND CENTRAL
PUBLISHING

NEW YORK   BOSTON

Copyright © 2017 by Kimberla Lawson Roby
Reading group guide copyright © 2017 by Kimberla Lawson Roby and Hachette Book Group, Inc.
Cover design by Elizabeth Connor. Photograph of locket © Michael Haegele/Getty Images. Woman's profile © Essl/Shutterstock. Woman's hairdo © Sarah Nicholl/Dreamstime.com.
Cover copyright © 2017 by Hachette Book Group, Inc.

Grand Central Publishing
Hachette Book Group
1290 Avenue of the Americas, New York, NY 10104
grandcentralpublishing.com
twitter.com/grandcentralpub

First Edition: January 2017

Grand Central Publishing is a division of Hachette Book Group, Inc. The Grand Central Publishing name and logo is a trademark of Hachette Book Group, Inc.

The publisher is not responsible for websites (or their content) that are not owned by the publisher.

The Hachette Speakers Bureau provides a wide range of authors for speaking events. To find out more, go to www.hachettespeakersbureau.com or call (866) 376-6591.

Library of Congress Cataloging-in-Publication Data
Names: Roby, Kimberla Lawson, author.
Title: Copycat / Kimberla Lawson Roby.
Description: First edition. | New York : Grand Central Publishing, 2017.
Identifiers: LCCN 2016028883| ISBN 9781455569717 (hardcover) |
ISBN 9781478967507 (audio download) | ISBN 9781478968856 (audio CD) |
ISBN 9781455569724 (ebook)
Subjects: | BISAC: FICTION / African American / Contemporary Women.
Classification: LCC PS3568.O3189 C67 2017 | DDC 813/.54—dc23 LC record available at https://lccn.loc.gov/2016028883

ISBNs: 978-1-4555-6971-7 (hardcover), 978-1-4555-6972-4 (ebook)

Printed in the United States of America

LSC-C

10 9 8 7 6 5 4 3 2 1

Cop•y•cat / ˈkäpēˌkat

A person who copies another's behavior, dress, or ideas.

"Believe in God, believe in yourself, believe in whatever it is you are trying to accomplish...believe in that order."

~ Kimberla Lawson Roby ~

In memory of the best agent ever... Elaine Koster.
September 8, 1940 – August 10, 2010

Though I wish you were still here in person to witness
the release of my 25th book, I know you are with me
in spirit. Thank you for believing in me from the very
beginning... thank you for everything.

Copycat

Chapter 1

Simone walked inside Marie's Hair Salon and stopped dead in her tracks. She wasn't positive, but she could've sworn that Traci Calloway Cole, the nationally known author, was sitting in the waiting area. She knew Traci lived in Mitchell, yet she'd never seen her in person.

Simone stepped closer to the smiling twentysomething receptionist. "Hi, I have a five forty-five appointment with Renee."

"Of course," the young woman said, typing on her computer keyboard. "It looks like Renee has already done a consult with you by phone, so I think you're all set. She should be with you shortly, but in the meantime, would you like coffee or tea? We also have bottled water."

"No, I think I'm fine for now, but maybe later."

"Sounds good. You can have a seat right over there," the receptionist said, eyeing the waiting area.

"Thank you."

Simone sat across from the woman she believed to be Traci Calloway Cole, and once they made eye contact, she knew it was her. Simone had seen her photo on her book jackets and on her web site, and she looked just like it: same thick, shoulder-length hair, high cheekbones, and all.

Traci smiled. "How are you?"

"I'm good, and you?"

"Doing well."

Simone set her brown shoulder bag on the chair next to her. "I hope it's okay for me to ask, but are you Traci Calloway Cole?"

Traci smiled again. "Yeah, that would be me I guess."

They both laughed.

"Well, I'm Simone Phillips, and it's very nice to meet you."

"It's nice to meet you as well."

Simone didn't want to show it, but she was ecstatic—especially since she'd written a book herself and had been hoping she would soon meet a published author in person. "I have both your books, and I really enjoyed reading them."

"How very kind of you, and thank you. I really appreciate that."

"You're quite welcome. I had also planned on attending both your signings, but when your first book came out I was ill. Then when your other one was released last year, I was out of town."

"Well, I hope you can come in September. That's when my next book is being published."

"I'll be there."

Traci set down the magazine she was holding. "So, have you been coming here for a while?"

"No, as a matter of fact, this is my first time. But I've heard really great things about it. What about you?"

"Marie has been my hairstylist for fifteen years. She didn't

2

open her salon until five years ago, but I went to her when she worked with someone else. She's very talented, and she's good people. One of the sweetest women I know."

"That's wonderful. And actually, my appointment is with Renee."

"Renee is awesome as well, and you'll love her, too. To be honest, I think you'd be happy with any of the stylists here. All of them take their work very seriously, and they have the best customer service."

"That's one of the reasons I decided to give them a try. A girl at work raved over how well they treat their clients."

"It's the truth. They never overbook, and you never have to wait longer than five or ten minutes when you arrive. Your appointment is your appointment and no one else's."

"Well, I wish I could say the same for the salon I've patronized for more than two years. There have been times when my stylist would schedule three other people around the same time she scheduled me, and I never got out of there until three hours after my appointment. But it was two weeks ago, when I had a six p.m. appointment and didn't get out until after ten, that I was finally done. I knew I was never going back there."

Traci raised her eyebrows. "Four hours? Did you get a relaxer? Color? Something that would justify being there all that time?"

"No, that's the killing part about all of it. Yes, there were two other clients and my stylist was trying to work on all three of us, but all I got was a wash, blow dry, and curl. That's it."

"How awful. I just don't get that. I realize everyone wants

to earn as much as possible, but it doesn't make much sense if you end up losing all your clients. Nowadays people have a lot of choices, and they can take their business elsewhere."

"Exactly," Simone said, looking around the salon. "When I first walked in, I wondered where everyone was. I mean, you and I are the only two waiting."

"That's because Marie and Renee are finishing up their clients right as we speak, and the other three stylists just started on theirs."

"I love it here already. And it's so chic looking."

"After what *you've* been through, I guess so," Traci said, and they both laughed. "But where did you go before you found your last stylist?"

"A place called Seasons."

"I've heard of it, but I've never gone there."

"It was nice enough, but I wasn't really happy with the way my hair usually turned out. Or at least it never turned out the way it always had when I lived in Ohio. The girl I went to there was an expert on working with short styles," Simone said, now regretting that she'd slipped and mentioned where she was from. It wasn't that this information was a secret, but Ohio was a place she tried not to think about.

"You really do have a cute cut. It's very becoming."

"Thanks."

"And is that where you're from? Ohio?"

"Yes."

"Really? Then how did you end up here in Mitchell?" Traci said, chuckling. "Don't get me wrong, I love my hometown and I wouldn't live anywhere else, but most people who move here come for a reason."

Simone laughed along with her. "I'm sure, because it's not like it's a major city."

"Far from it. A hundred fifty thousand people isn't tiny, but it's still small."

"The insurance company I work for closed that location, and in order for me to keep my position and seniority, I had to take an opening here."

"Oh, okay."

Simone still hated that she'd had to relocate so abruptly, but in truth, it couldn't have come at a better time. So much had happened, most of which she tried to block from her mind on a daily basis. Life in Ohio had turned out terribly, and she would never forgive her former fiancé, who'd purposely betrayed her. He'd turned on her and told things he shouldn't have to the wrong people. But that was a whole other story, and thankfully, it was all behind her.

Simone and Traci chatted a couple of minutes longer until Marie walked toward them.

"Ready?" the tall, shapely woman said to Traci.

"Yep, and by the way, this is Simone. This is her first time coming here, and she has an appointment with Renee."

"That's great. Welcome, and please let us know if you need anything or if there's something we can do better for you."

"I will, and thank you."

Traci grabbed her Gucci shoulder bag and stood up. "It was very nice meeting you, Simone. I really enjoyed talking to you."

"Likewise, and much continued success with your books."

"Thank you."

When Traci and Marie walked away, Simone could barely

contain herself. Traci was so nice, outgoing, and down-to-earth. She was also beautiful, and Simone loved the dark denim skinny jeans and oversized fuchsia cashmere sweater she had on. It was exactly the kind of outfit she'd love to have herself, and the black heeled boots Traci wore were to die for.

Now Simone wished she'd had the courage to tell Traci about the romance novel she'd written. She'd desperately wanted to, but she hadn't wanted Traci to think that this was the only reason she'd introduced herself. Sometimes that sort of thing could be a turnoff, when all a person wanted was to relax, have a cordial conversation, and not talk about work. Simone certainly understood that, and she respected people's time.

Simone picked up a copy of *Essence* magazine from the glass table in front of her, but when she did, she saw a woman walking toward the receptionist to make payment and another heading in her direction.

"You must be Simone?" the petite middle-aged woman said.

"I am. Are you Renee?"

"Yes, and it's a pleasure to meet you."

They shook hands, and Simone said, "It's a pleasure to meet you also."

Renee turned to the side. "I'm all ready for you."

"Sounds good."

Simone followed Renee, and as she passed Traci, sitting in one of Marie's chairs, Traci smiled at her and said, "Enjoy."

"I will," Simone replied, and it was then that she made up her mind to contact Traci for advice on writing and how to get published. She was also going to make some changes in her wardrobe; see if she could find those jeans and that sweater Traci was wearing. She'd even love to have Traci's boots, but with it already being the first week in March, pickings for boots were likely pretty slim. Although, when it came to the Gucci purse Traci was carrying, Simone knew she could purchase that as soon as possible—just as soon as she drove over to Chicago to the Gucci store on Michigan Avenue. She would do so the second she got off work tomorrow.

Chapter 2

Traci drove her white double-sunroof Mercedes into the subdivision, heading toward the street she and Tim lived on. As she turned into the driveway and pressed the button in her car to open the garage, she gazed at their five-thousand-square-foot brick home. Traci thanked God for all that He'd blessed her and her husband with, because things had certainly been very different for her eighteen years ago. Right after college, she'd married her high school sweetheart—if that was what a person could call it—and the whole scenario had been a nightmare. She'd known early on that he'd become a bit too possessive and controlling, but at twenty-two, she hadn't taken these obvious warning signs very seriously. She'd decided that many of his actions "weren't that bad," and that with time, he'd get used to the fact that she had goals, dreams, and ambitions—that he would eventually understand that these goals, dreams, and ambitions meant they could both have a better life.

But for whatever reason, he'd never made any changes, and instead of getting better, things had gotten worse—starting with their wedding night, when he'd turned his back to her in bed and never touched her, all because he'd insisted that she'd spent their wedding day staring at one of his groomsmen. This, of course, couldn't have been further from the truth, and it had literally been the beginning of the end. They'd dated for five years, but it had only taken three months of marriage for Traci's ex-husband to put his hands on her and convincingly threaten her life. However, it was when he'd taken a pillow one night and pressed it over her face—because she wouldn't "shut up" the way he'd told her—that she'd realized enough was enough. Her realization had been long overdue, but somehow, seeing her life flash before her eyes had been the ultimate wake-up call, and she'd left him fast and in a hurry. But nonetheless, he'd continued to harass her, even after she'd gotten a judge to sign a restraining order, and it had been only by the grace of God that when their divorce had become final, he'd left her alone for good.

Today, though, life was better than ever, and it was all because fifteen years ago she'd met an amazing man named Timothy Cole, who she'd immediately known was her soul mate for life. Tim, as she'd always called him, had felt the same way, and they'd married six months after their first date. Of course, everyone had thought they were crazy, but the two of them had felt good about each other, and today, their love was even stronger than it was back then.

Traci pulled into the garage, turned off her ignition, and lifted her phone from the passenger seat. She saw notification of a Facebook inbox message and opened it. She smiled when she realized it was from Simone, the woman she'd just met this evening at the hair salon.

Hi Traci,

I first want to say how it really was a pleasure to meet you, and that I hope it's okay that I'm contacting you. I'm sure you get notes all the time from aspiring writers, which is why I was so hesitant about sending you a message, but I decided that I was simply going to take a chance. Especially since you were so kind and approachable, and when you left the salon, Marie and Renee were saying how you've always been that way. That you're the same person you were before you ever had a book published.

Anyway, the reason I'm contacting you is because I've written a romance novel entitled LOVE NEVER FAILS. I just finished it last month, and the story centers on a man and a woman who fall in love, but then they lose touch with each other when the man is sent overseas with the military for three years. He loves her with all his heart, but sadly, he insists that he doesn't want her feeling obligated to wait on him, and he ends their relationship. However, when he returns injured, their paths cross again, except now the woman is married to an unloving man she can barely stand, even though she does still love her former boyfriend.

What I'm hoping is that you can find it in your heart to give me some advice on finding a literary agent and/or publisher. I have read a couple of writing self-help books, but I also know that some of the best advice a person can receive is the kind that comes from someone who is already doing what you want to do careerwise. And don't get me wrong, I know I'm asking a lot, particularly since I know you must have a very busy schedule and because you don't really know me, so if you don't have time, I will totally understand. It's just that, ever since high school, my top goal in life has been to become a published writer.

Oh, and if you do find that you have time to offer some advice and it would be quicker for you to do it by phone, that would be great also. I'll add my cell number below, and once again, it really was an honor to meet you. It made my day.

Thank you, and I hope to talk with you soon.
Simone

Traci didn't see where Simone had left her phone number, but then she saw another inbox message pop in, with Simone apologizing for forgetting to include it. She'd made sure to add it this time around, and Traci was glad because she already liked Simone, not to mention she tried her best to help as many new writers as possible. So once she and Tim had dinner, she was going to call Simone to chat with her about her book.

When Traci cleared her and Tim's dishes from the island, she took them over to the sink and rinsed them off. But as soon as she prepared to load them in the dishwasher, Tim walked up behind her and wrapped his arms around her.

Then he kissed her on her neck. "You know what I want, right?"

Traci laughed. "Tim, will you stop it. Because if you don't, I'll leak water all over the floor."

"I think you should take care of those dishes later," he said, kissing her neck again. "Don't you?"

"Well, actually, I told a new writer that I would call her this evening."

"Wow," Tim said, now kissing the other side of her neck. "I guess I know how I rate around here, don't I?"

Traci turned and looked at him, playfully rolling her eyes. "You know that's not true. It's just that I know what it feels like, wanting to be published and not being able to find one published writer who will answer even a single question. But I promise you, baby, I won't be on very long."

Tim kissed her cheek and took a couple of steps back. "You know I'm just kidding, anyway. I love that you want to help other writers, so you can be on with her for as long as you need to. But just know, though, that I'll be ready and waiting as soon as you finish."

"Yeah, I'm sure you will," she said, laughing, and Tim did, too.

He turned and walked away, jokingly ignoring her. "See you in the bedroom."

Traci watched him disappear down the corridor toward their master suite, which was also on the first floor. He was ten years her senior, but he was as handsome as ever. He was also fun and full of energy, sometimes even more so than she was. The man acted as though he were never tired, not even after a full day's work, but this was yet one more thing Traci loved about her husband. There was never a dull moment, and she was grateful for that—she was grateful for him.

After finishing up in the kitchen, Traci went upstairs to her home office, which she'd converted from a guest bedroom, and sat at her desk. She signed on to Facebook, wrote down Simone's phone number, and dialed it.

She answered on the first ring. "Hello?"

"Simone?"

"Yes."

"Hey, this is Traci. Did I catch you at a bad time?"

"No, not at all, and thank you so, so much for calling me. I can't believe you had time to talk right away tonight."

"You're quite welcome. Also, how did your hair turn out? Did you like Renee and the way she styled it?"

"I love it. She did such a great job, and I'll definitely be going back to her."

"Wonderful. I knew you'd be happy."

"Calling to make an appointment was the best thing I could've done."

"So," Traci said, "you mentioned in your message that you've wanted to write since high school."

"I have. I took a creative writing class, and from the first day, I knew I wanted to write fiction. In the beginning, I was just thinking short stories, but it wasn't long before my dream was to write a novel. Actually, a romance novel. So what about you?"

"I knew when I was in high school, too, that I wanted to have a career in writing, but I wasn't sure if I wanted to write books or magazine articles. I also loved my journalism classes, so there was a time when I wanted to be a news anchor. But by the time I finished college, I knew that my purpose in life was to write novels. Especially mainstream women's fiction."

"Wow, I can't believe we have the whole high school thing in common," Simone said.

Traci leaned back in her chair. "Yeah, I know, but look how long it took me to get published. I turned forty in January, and my first book wasn't published until two years ago."

"Well, it's taken me even longer, but oh my good-ness...did you say forty? I turned forty last week."

"Really?"

"Yes, so I guess we have that in common, too."

"I guess so," Traci agreed. "Did you do anything special for your birthday?"

"No, not really. Did you?"

"My sister put together a girls' trip with some friends of ours, and we celebrated in Florida."

"I'll bet that was nice."

"It was. So hey, how far along are you with your book? I know you said you'd finished writing it, but have you already gotten it edited and proofed?"

"No, I haven't done anything. But I would definitely like to hire a freelance editor."

"I can give you some names of content editors, copyeditors, and proofreaders, because before it's all done, you'll need all three."

"Sounds good."

"After that, you should start writing query letters to send out to agents. You can try submitting directly to editors at publishing houses, but if you can sign with a reputable agent, your chances of getting published will be that much better."

"That's what I've heard, and I appreciate anything you can do to help me."

"My agent doesn't represent romance, but I can certainly ask her for the names of agents who do."

"How kind of you. You would actually do that?"

"Of course. I mean, I know I can't promise anything, but at least I can get the names of the right people."

"I will never be able to thank you enough, Traci."

"I'm glad to do it."

"I just don't know what to say. Because I'm sure you must be very busy."

"I am, and sometimes that stops me from helping as many people as I would like. But you seem like a really nice person who has such a strong passion for writing. And I love that."

"I do. I love writing more than anything. And if I didn't have a full-time job, I would write day and night."

"I remember when I felt the same way. Especially back in my twenties, but then when I kept getting rejected, I basically gave up. I mean, I still wrote, but I didn't submit anything again for almost ten years."

"Well, I'm glad you finally decided to give it another try, because I love your stories. And I love your writing style."

"Thank you for saying that. Especially since I can think of a few writers who believe I never should've been published," Traci said, laughing. "That really used to bother me, but not anymore. Now all I care about is what my readers think, and I ignore mean-spirited authors. Some actually believe it's their job to criticize every author's work—except their own, that is."

"That's really too bad. It's so unfortunate that folks just can't be happy for their colleagues."

Traci nodded as though Simone were in the room with her. "Sadly, this happens in every industry. More so with women. But don't get me wrong, not all writers are like that. Some are very kind, and they root for me as much as I root for them. But for the most part, I pretty much stay to myself. I had to start doing that versus listening to negative, unsupportive people who only want to bring others down."

"I don't blame you, and you're right about it happening in every industry, because the same thing goes on where I work. I've worked with insurance claims for years, but until I came to Mitchell I'd never experienced so much competitiveness. And cattiness. It's fine, though, because I've gotten used to it."

"Good for you."

"Well, hey," Simone said. "I really appreciate your calling me, but I don't want to take up any more of your time."

"I'm glad we got to talk this evening, and let's connect again in a few days."

"Sounds good. I can also email you two or three chapters if you want to read them. You know, just to make sure my work is even good enough to be hiring an editor."

"Sure, that's fine," Traci said, but she sort of wished Simone hadn't asked her to do that. Not because she didn't want to read her work, but because writing was so subjective and what Traci might consider a page-turner, someone else might think was the worst book they'd read. Similarly, a novel that Traci didn't care for at all might end up selling millions of copies. So she just didn't feel as though it was her place to say, which was the reason she much preferred only giving advice on how to find an agent or how to get published. But she could tell Simone truly did want her to read her work, and after all, it was only three chapters.

"Traci, thank you again. Thank you for everything."

"You're quite welcome. Have a good night."

"You too."

Chapter 3

Simone still couldn't believe it. She'd actually met Traci Calloway Cole, and better than that, she'd just gotten off the phone with her. *And* Traci had agreed to help her. *And* she was going to read the first three chapters of Simone's book. *And* she'd given Simone her personal email address. It all seemed much too good to be true, but it wasn't, and Simone hadn't felt this excited in a long time. Of course, she would have to proofread her chapters at least three or four more times before sending them to Traci; however, she couldn't wait to hear her feedback.

Simone pulled up Traci's web site and browsed through every page again—the same as she'd done at least ten other times since arriving home this evening. But when she clicked on her bio page again, she studied the fuchsia silk blouse Traci wore in her official author photo. It was interesting because earlier at the hair salon, Traci had been wearing a fuchsia sweater, which meant she obviously had a strong love for this particular color. Simone had never worn much fuchsia or hot pink, but it was actually more beautiful than she'd realized. So she opened another Google window and searched

17

the words "women's fuchsia blouses." She started with Macy's and continued on to the web sites of Nordstrom, Lord & Taylor, Dillard's, Saks Fifth Avenue, White House Black Market, Ann Taylor, and Talbots. When she still couldn't find the exact blouse that Traci wore in the photo, she settled on the closest one she'd found at Saks. At three hundred dollars, it was a bit on the pricey side, but she just couldn't pass on buying it. She wanted it, and if she was going to look as though she were a published author, it was a sacrifice she needed to make. A sacrifice she *had* to make. Not to mention, it was a very necessary investment in her career.

Simone added the blouse to her shopping cart, and since she'd never purchased from Saks before, she created an online account. Then she changed the shipping selection from standard to Saturday delivery. This selection, of course, was costing her an additional thirty-five dollars. It would have been at least ten dollars less for regular overnight delivery, but with it being this late on Thursday, her package wouldn't go out until tomorrow and then wouldn't arrive until the next business day on Monday. But she didn't want to wait until then.

When the order had been confirmed, Simone clicked away from Saks and returned to Traci's web site. She saw Traci's live Twitter feed displaying on the home page and scrolled through it to see what Traci had recently tweeted or what comments of others she had retweeted. Then she clicked on Traci's Twitter photos. As Simone browsed through them, something she'd already done about an hour ago, she wished she'd already been published and now had the loyal readers Traci had. Her events seemed well attended, and Simone could tell from every photo Traci took with readers that she genuinely loved them and was having the time of her life.

If only Simone had taken her writing more seriously and had majored in English or creative writing, she would be so much further along than she was. She'd never have had to take a job at an insurance company, and she certainly wouldn't still be working for one now. She'd be living the same kind of life she was sure Traci was living. She hadn't seen Traci's home, but Simone could just about imagine what it looked like. She was also pretty sure that the white Mercedes S550 she'd seen in the hair salon's parking lot was Traci's. It was true that Marie, the owner of the salon, was doing very well for herself and that the Mercedes might belong to her, but Simone was betting her money on Traci. She just had a feeling about it, and now she wished she had purchased a Mercedes herself instead of the black Nissan Maxima she owned. An S550 was certainly far more than she could afford, but just having a white Mercedes of any kind would work for her. She'd always sort of liked white vehicles, anyway, but after seeing the car she believed to be Traci's, she knew it was an amazing color to have.

When the doorbell rang, Simone forced her eyes away from her computer and got up. She walked down the hallway to the front door and reached for the knob.

"Who is it?"

"It's me, baby."

Simone opened the door for her fiancé, Chris, and smiled.

"Hey, gorgeous," he said, hugging her and kissing her on the lips. "How are you?"

"I'm good, and you?"

"Great," he said, kissing her again. "Especially now that I'm here with my girl."

"I was just sitting in my office," she said, turning to head back in that direction.

Chris followed behind her. Simone didn't look back at him, but from the time they'd met, she'd loved how handsome he was. She'd immediately been attracted to his chiseled six-foot-two frame and flawless skin, and the chemistry between them had been near instant.

They walked inside Simone's home office, and when she sat back in front of her computer Chris took a seat next to her desk, facing her. But now he stared at her.

She looked back at him. "What?"

"I'm just wondering how much longer it's going to be before you give me a key."

"Soon."

"You've been saying that since we got engaged, and that was three months ago."

"I know, but I just need you to be patient."

"I still don't understand your hesitation, especially when we're getting married next year. Plus, I've offered you the key to my place more than once."

"I realize that, but I can't help how I feel. I know you don't get it, but until we finish pre-marital counseling with your pastor I want us to keep things as is."

"But you see, that's what's so confusing," he said. "You never go to church, but you wanted us to attend these sessions with Pastor Raymond."

"I did, and I'm glad we're doing it. I'm not into the idea of religion, but I do believe in God. And the one time I went to church with you, I liked what your pastor had to say."

Chris rolled his eyes toward the ceiling, obviously still not understanding, and Simone wished she could let her guard down and confide in him more. But she couldn't. Not when she'd been engaged once before, and things hadn't worked out. She'd trusted her former fiancé completely, but he'd betrayed her in a way she hadn't thought possible. She loved Chris, and deep down a part of her did trust him, but another part of her needed a bit more confirmation that he was the real deal and that he was fully committed to her. It wasn't that he'd done anything wrong or anything to make her doubt him, but she still had to be careful. She couldn't let what happened with her last fiancé happen in this relationship. She'd been so devastated, she pretended that she'd never been engaged at all or lived in Ohio. It was just better that way. Better to focus on the new life she'd been able to create for herself right here in Mitchell. Better to live a brand-new life with a different set of coworkers in a different city with different friends.

Chris picked up a magazine from her desk, thumbing through it, but he didn't say anything else.

Simone reached over and rested her hand under his chin. "Baby, please don't be mad. Try to understand."

"I *am* trying. And the only reason I'm going along with this is because I love you."

"I love you, too, and I promise you things won't always be this way."

Chris glanced over at Simone's computer screen. "Who's that?"

"You won't believe this, but when I was at that new hair salon earlier I met Traci Calloway Cole. You know, the local author you've heard me talk about?"

"Really? And that's her web site?"

"Yep."

"Did you tell her you'd written a book, too?"

"I did, but not until I got home and sent her a message. And she already called me."

"That's great."

"She's also going to answer any questions I have and read some of my chapters."

"That's even better, and I hope she can help you get published," he said, pulling her out of her chair, gazing into her eyes, and hugging her again.

Simone wrapped her arms around his waist. "I do, too. I want that more than anything."

"And I'm sure it'll happen," he said, kissing her.

Then he took her hand and led her toward her bedroom. Simone had been hoping they could talk more about her conversation with Traci, but it was obvious that Chris had other plans for them. She knew he wanted to make love to her, and in all honesty, the feeling was mutual.

Chapter 4

$\mathcal{T}$he last place Simone wanted to be right now was at work, but that's exactly where she was. Still, as she sat in her office with the door closed, she certainly wasn't reviewing any insurance claims. Instead, she'd just finished proofreading the first three chapters of her manuscript, and currently, she was signed on to Twitter, checking to see what Traci had posted this morning. She scrolled down to today's first entry, which said, "This is the day which the Lord hath made; we will rejoice and be glad in it. ~ Psalm 118:24 (KJV) Happy Friday, and have a great weekend!"

"What a really great idea," Simone said out loud, and then she clicked to Google and searched the phrase "great scriptures to start your day." She didn't know a lot about the Bible, but it didn't take long for her to find a verse she liked. When she did, she signed back on to Twitter, this time to her own page, and typed: "Trust in the LORD with all thine heart; and lean not unto thine own understanding."

But as soon as she hit Enter, she realized that she hadn't included the squiggly symbol, which book of the Bible she was referencing, the verse number, or the source of scripture

23

interpretation, the way Traci had. So she hurried to delete her tweet and retyped it, this time including "~ Proverbs 3:5 (KJV)." She also told her followers to enjoy their weekend.

Simone reread her tweet, making sure there weren't any typos, and then returned to Traci's page. She clicked on Traci's Twitter photos, and when she saw a graphic of Traci's next novel, she knew right then and there that she wanted her first jacket to look exactly like it, or at the very least, as close as possible. She was sure that whatever publisher she signed with would have an art department responsible for this sort of thing, but having a design like Traci's would make all the difference. Traci's readers already loved her books, and if they saw a similar design for her jacket, they would want to read Simone's just because of it.

Simone's phone rang, and although she knew it was likely a customer calling, she ignored it. This was, of course, one of the benefits of having a closed-door office, and Simone was grateful for that. When it stopped ringing, Simone scrolled back to the top of Traci's Twitter page and saw that she had five more followers than she'd had last night...already. Simone had purposely checked the number, which had been 10,307, and now it was 10,312. Simone was lucky if she gained five followers in a week or sometimes in a month, and she had to do something to change that. As it was, she only had seventy-three, and those were mostly coworkers she didn't like and a few strangers who'd randomly followed her in hopes that she would follow them back—people whose main goal in life was to gain as many social media followers as possible. Before yesterday, Simone had never cared one way or the other, but after seeing that Traci had ten thousand plus, she knew it was time for her to up her game—it was high time she got on the ball and did all she could to get her name out there; not as Simone Phillips the auto insurance claims specialist but as Simone Phillips, aspiring writer and future bestselling author.

Simone's phone rang again, and she frowned. Then, when she looked over at the caller ID screen, she sighed. Freda Jamison was the customer from hell, the queen of Hades, and she was the last person Simone wanted to talk to. Freda's insurance policy had been canceled, and rightfully so, but she wasn't taking no for an answer. So Simone let the phone ring until it stopped.

Simone knew she needed to get back to work, and she would…just as soon as she Googled Traci's name and clicked on the images. She browsed all the different photos of her that displayed, and she could tell that Traci always wore her thick, shoulder-length hair down and very loosely curled. Simone didn't see one shot where she'd worn it up or back in a ponytail, and suddenly Simone wished she'd allowed her own hair to grow out. She'd always loved wearing extra-short haircuts, but for the first time, she wanted something a little different. She'd also never worn extensions, but now she was very much open to the idea. Long, thick hair seemed much more becoming for an author or any public icon, and Simone needed to make some changes to her appearance. Lots of them.

When Simone's phone rang again, she sighed in a huff. "What?" she said to herself as she looked over and saw that it was Freda. Still, she didn't answer it. But not two minutes later, the receptionist called and Simone knew she needed to pick up the phone.

"This is Simone speaking."

"Hi, Simone. I have a Freda Jamison on the line for you. She says she left you three messages yesterday and called you three more times this morning and really needs to speak to you."

Simone cringed. "Please put her through."

"Will do," the receptionist replied. "Thanks so much."

Simone took a deep breath. "Good morning, how can I help you?"

"It's about time," Freda bellowed out. "Because I know you saw me calling. I'm not stupid. Big companies now have caller ID screens just like anyone else."

Simone pretended she hadn't heard a word of what this woman was saying. "What can I do for you, Mrs. Jamison?"

"You know exactly what you can do. Reinstate my policy."

"I'm sorry, but we can't do that."

"What you mean is that you *won't.*"

"No, I mean we can't."

"Why?"

Simone shook her head. Only two days ago, she'd gone out of her way to explain everything to Freda, yet here she was asking her what she already knew. "Not only have we covered two other accidents that required the repair of your car and those of the people you collided with, but both accidents were your fault. You were ticketed both times. But we're still going to cover this third accident as well."

"Then I don't see the problem."

"The problem is that even though we're covering you this one last time, we've had to end our relationship with you. We can no longer cover someone who's had three accidents in less than two years. I'm sure you can understand that."

"Excuse me? Sweetheart, if I understood it, I wouldn't be wasting my time on this phone with you."

Simone didn't say anything.

"Hello?" the woman yelled. "Are you there?"

"I'm here, but I'm not sure what else I can say."

"You're a real piece of work, and if you can't reinstate my policy, I'll have to call your boss. Someone who has some real say-so over there. Someone who won't be happy when he or she hears how I've been treated."

Simone almost wanted to laugh. So now Freda was threatening her? Please. "Do you want me to transfer you? Because it's certainly not a problem. To be honest, I'd be more than happy to do it."

There was silence, and Simone knew Freda hadn't expected the answer she'd gotten.

"Hello?" Simone said.

"No, you little heifer, I'll make the call myself."

Simone raised her eyebrows, but before she could respond, Freda hung up on her. Simone couldn't stand dealing with irate customers, and even more so when they were completely in the wrong. Freda was lucky they hadn't canceled her policy after the second accident, what with the level of damage that had been done and the amount of money they'd had to spend to fix everything. But here she was livid because they weren't allowing her the opportunity to hit yet a fourth vehicle somewhere down the road.

Simone looked back at her computer, and although she'd spent much of her morning focusing on everything but her job responsibilities, she took another look at Traci's public-figure Facebook page. Traci had posted a graphic of her new book, a buy link for preordering it, and another link so readers could read the first couple of chapters. Over here, she had 25,117 followers, which was more than twice the followers she had on Twitter, and more than five hundred people had clicked "Like" on each status update. On top of that, fifty of them had written some amazing comments: "I'm not reading the first two chapters when all it's going to do is make me spend the next few months wishing I could read the rest." "I just read the excerpt you posted, and now my heart is racing a mile a minute! I so can't wait for September to get here!" "How dare you post two chapters, knowing it will be six months before we can even buy the actual book! Shame on you, Traci, for doing this to us! LOL!" "Ms. Traci. I'm a senior in high school and when my mom bought me both your books for Christmas, I read them in two days, back to back. So I literally can't wait for your next one to be released. My mom can't wait either!"

Simone admired the love and support that Traci was receiving from her readers, but she also wanted to experience this for herself. She wanted her book to be published, she wanted it to make as many bestseller lists as possible, and she wanted to make a good living from it. She didn't want to be rich, but she did want to be financially comfortable. She also wanted to be as well-known as Traci. Simone could already tell that she and Traci had great chemistry and a lot of the same tastes when it came to clothes, boots, and cars—which was the reason she'd changed her mind about driving over to Chicago after work to pick up that Gucci purse. She'd known that taking the trip had meant she would physically have the bag in her possession by this evening, but for some reason, she hadn't been able to wait. So, instead, she'd pulled up Gucci's web site this morning, hours before getting dressed, and had placed her order. And as she'd done with the blouse she purchased from Saks last night, she'd chosen Saturday delivery.

But it wasn't just clothes, boots, and cars that Simone and Traci shared the same tastes for, because Simone had also discovered that they even liked the same hairstyle. It was true that Simone had never worn long hair, but it was only because she'd always been pretty set in her ways and hadn't realized that, like Traci, she loved shoulder-length hair. So Simone knew it would only be a matter of time before she saw her dreams come to pass. She just had to work hard at it and stay persistent. She would learn everything she could from Traci, and before long, she'd have a huge publishing contract—like Traci—and she'd be able to write full-time from now on...the same as Traci was.

Chapter 5

$\mathcal{T}$raci responded to a few business emails she'd received from her editor, her publicist, and a blogger who'd sent her interview questions she needed answered by next week. But because Traci preferred handling to-do items as soon as she could, she decided to answer the questions now. There were only five of them, so it wouldn't take her very long anyway.

When she finished, she reached for her office phone and called her literary agent.

She picked up after the second ring. "Helen Stone."

"Hi, Helen, it's Traci."

"Hi, Traci. How are you?"

"I'm doing well. You?"

"Doing great. So what's up?"

"Well, I met a new writer yesterday. Simone Phillips. And she's written her first romance novel. I know you don't represent that genre, but I was wondering if you could recommend someone else."

"Yes, absolutely. There are actually two that she should definitely contact. Both are excellent at what they do, and they

30

represent both new and veteran romance writers. Some have written twenty or more books and many have *New York Times* bestsellers."

"This is wonderful, and I know it will be very helpful."

"Tanny Matthews is one, and the other is Michaela Vander-bilt. They'll expect to receive the standard query letter rather than initial chapters, and your friend can find their contact information on their web sites."

"Sounds good."

"I wish I could be of more help, but without reading her work myself, I can't personally call and recommend her to Tanny and Michaela."

"I understand."

"Actually, I don't know if I've ever told you why I don't represent romance."

"No, I don't think you have. I just knew you didn't."

"Well, it's not that I don't think it would do well for me, because in all honestly, romance sells more than half of all fiction. And sometimes I love reading a good romance story. But I'm also much more of a contemporary and women's fiction reader, and I believe that the best agents represent the kinds of books they would read all the time, even if they weren't agents. In other words, they best represent books they love the most and have the strongest passion for."

"That makes perfect sense."

"It's the same thing for editors. The only way editors can truly edit a book to the best of their ability is when they love, love, love the author's writing style and genre. Otherwise, it's impossible to have a true connection to the work. And when that happens, they can't always champion the book or the author to higher-ups in their publishing company."

"Very interesting, and I definitely agree. I also think that this philosophy holds true for any job. The more passion you have for what you do, the better you'll be at it."

"Some agents represent all genres because they want the business. But again, if they don't love the work it doesn't always benefit the author."

"I can certainly see where it wouldn't. And we all know what happens when folks become jacks-of-all-trades."

"Yes, masters of none. But the good news, missy, is that you don't have that problem," Helen said with a smile in her voice.

"No, I can tell I don't, and I'm really grateful to you for that. You have been a writer's dream, and you also sold my books to the best editor ever. Someone who cares about my work and me. I also love everything that Ford represents," she said, referring to her publisher, Ford-Anderson Press, "and a person just couldn't ask for anything more than that."

"Well, you're quite welcome. You're a joy to work with, and I only want the best for you. And speaking of which, I just want to say again how much I enjoyed reading *Copycat*."

"I'm so glad, and I really think a lot of women will be able to relate to it."

"I agree. I've always known that some women like mimicking others, such as a close friend or sister, but I think *your* book will get women talking about it much more openly."

"That's my hope. Thankfully, I don't have any friends who do this kind of thing, but I've definitely come across women

who have identity problems. Those who want to be like someone else."

"It happens more than I think most of us realize, so I'm
glad you decided to tackle this subject."

"I'm glad, too."

"Your readers are definitely going to enjoy it, and I can already imagine what some of the book club discussions will be
like. Especially if club members have dealt with a copycat of
some kind."

"Well, I guess we'll see soon enough, because September
is only six months away."

"Time is flying, but things are coming together very
nicely—thanks to the number of copies that were sold of your
second book. Sales were fifty percent higher than your first
novel, and because of that, Ford is sending you on a ten-city
tour this time and increasing your marketing and advertising
budgets. It's also still pretty early, yet your readers have already begun preordering."

"I'm really hoping *Copycat* does well."

"I believe it will, and I'm excited for you. I also can't wait
to see what you're planning next."

"I'm almost finished with my synopsis, so I'll be sending it
to you soon."

"Good, because with the way things are going, I wouldn't
be surprised at all if Ford offered you a three- or four-book
deal this time."

"You think?"

"I do. An increase in sales can mean everything."

"That's what I've heard."

"This is going to be a great year for you. I can feel it already."

Traci smiled, and without warning, tears filled her eyes. "I'll never be able to thank you enough, Helen. You took a chance on me when no one else would, and I am forever grateful to you for that. I'll never forget all that you've done for me."

"You're quite welcome, and this is only the beginning."

Traci got up and walked toward her office window. "Oh and hey, how is Rick doing?"

"He's coming along fine," Helen said about her husband. "Still hard to believe he just had open-heart surgery, but his doctor says he's recovering much better than expected. Getting stronger every day."

"This is such great news, and I'm praying for him daily."

"We really appreciate that. And how are Tim and your parents?"

"They're all doing well. Tim got the promotion I'd told you about, the marketing VP one, so we're pretty excited."

"As you should be. Please tell him I said congratulations."

"I will."

"Okay, then, I'm going to head out for a meeting now. You enjoy your day, though."

"You too, and thanks again for the agent information."

"Anytime, and please let me know how things turn out for your friend."

"Will do. Take care, Helen."

Chapter 6

*I*t was finally twelve noon, and while Simone would normally be raring to head out for her lunch break, the email she'd just received from Traci was all she could think about. So she sat there, rereading the names of the two literary agents Traci's agent had recommended. Simone also read the last part of the email again:

My agent says that both Tanny and Michaela do require query letters, but before I sent you this email, I checked their web sites for submission requirements and saw that both of them accept submissions electronically. I'm also looking forward to reading your chapters, so please send them when you're ready.

Have a great weekend!
Traci

Simone loved how personable and helpful Traci was, and as she glanced at Traci's Facebook page—this time her personal page and not her public one, which she'd now read postings for as far back as two years—she considered sending

Traci a friend request. Simone could tell that this particular page was protected with certain privacy settings, because she could only see a few old entries, but the more she stared at it, the more she wanted to see what else Traci had posted. She wanted the same access that Traci's close friends and family members had. Yes, Simone didn't know Traci well enough to necessarily connect with her on her personal page, but she also knew that many writers sometimes accepted friend requests from readers and new acquaintances.

Simone sat, debating back and forth. Should she or shouldn't she? Was she overstepping her bounds or wasn't she? Would Traci feel awkward about Simone sending her a request, or would she be happy about it? It was just too difficult to say one way or the other, so instead of making a final decision, Simone scrolled down Traci's page farther than she had earlier, checking out the few photos that were set for public viewing. And it was then that she saw a photo of Traci and a woman who looked to be Traci's mother. Simone wasn't positive, but with the exception of the woman being older than Traci, they looked almost like twins. They favored each other in every way, and they dressed in the same type of classy-looking clothes.

This just had to be Traci's mother, and when Simone clicked to read one of the comments under the photo, her assumption was confirmed: "It was such a pleasure meeting you, Traci, and I was also very honored to meet your sweet, beautiful mom. What an amazing lady. And of course, I can't wait to read your next book!"

Simone smiled at the kind words being said about Traci's mom, but then her face turned somber. The reason: she thought about her own mom, LeeAnn, and how awful her mother had been to her. LeeAnn had given birth to Simone when she was fifteen, but she'd also started using drugs a year later and hadn't stopped until about ten years ago. However, her recovery hadn't lasted. Simone knew this because when LeeAnn had contacted her three months ago, asking if she was planning to send her a Christmas gift, she'd sounded drunk, which likely meant she was now back on drugs.

She'd been a terrible mother who Simone hated for many reasons she still wept about, and because Simone's father had been killed in a robbery when she was two years old, she didn't remember him; which meant it felt as though she'd never had a father in the first place. Worse, her paternal grandparents hadn't wanted anything to do with Simone, and she didn't know who her maternal grandfather was, either. In other words, back in the day, Velma, Simone's maternal grandmother, had slept with a lot of men and had no clue who she'd conceived her only child with—that child being LeeAnn. Of course, it was true that Velma had taken custody of Simone and had raised her the best that she could, but she hadn't been a stellar example for her granddaughter. She'd actually been the worst role model a child could have, what with the way she'd continued to sleep with one man after another and had done so right in her own bedroom—the same room that shared a wall with the one Simone had slept in. Even when Simone had been only a small girl and was too young to fend for herself, she'd still been old enough to know that hearing her grandmother and all those men—doing whatever it was they'd been doing—wasn't right. Even now, she remembered all the loud moans and groans and cursing that had kept her wide awake until the wee hours of the morning, and she doubted she would ever be able to forget it.

Simone pondered her dreadful childhood until her cell phone rang. She half smiled when she saw that it was Chris, because he tended to make her feel better about everything.

"Hey, baby," he said. "How's it going?"

"Hey."

"What's wrong? You sound kind of down."

"No, I'm fine," she said, lying. "Just a busy morning here at work is all."

"Are you going to lunch?"

"No, I'll probably just get something from the cafeteria. You?"

"I'm headed to get a sandwich now."

Chris was a supervisor for the United States Postal Service and had been employed there for twenty years. He always talked about how he wished he'd gone to college, but he also earned nearly eighty thousand dollars a year; which was much more than she made with a four-year degree. Chris was also extremely responsible and wasn't fond of spending recklessly on unnecessary items, so he'd saved a lot of money, too.

Simone scrolled through more of Traci's Facebook page. "So where are you headed?"

"That little deli down the street from the post office. I didn't want to eat a lot because we're still going to dinner tonight, right?"

"Yep."

"And did you decide which movie you want to see?"

"No, but I will."

"Some really good ones were released today."

"I know, but right now, I need your opinion on something."

"What's that?"

"I'm thinking about sending Traci a friend request on Facebook."

"Traci who? The author you met?"

"Yes."

"Why?"

"I guess I just want to connect with her a lot more on social media."

"Why can't you just follow her on her public page? Because I'm sure she has one for readers."

"She does, and I already do."

"Then why do you need to be friends with her on her personal one?"

Simone sighed. "You don't get it."

"I guess I don't."

"She was really nice to me when I saw her yesterday and also when we spoke on the phone. Not to mention, she gave me her personal email address."

"That's all fine and well, but it's not like you really know her."

Simone didn't like how negative Chris was sounding and said, "I already thought about that."

"Then if I were you I'd wait until you guys got more acquainted."

Simone pretended she didn't hear his last comment.

"Are you there?" he asked.

"I'm here."

"But you don't like what I said, do you?"

"I'm fine."

"Okay, well, I'm almost at the deli, but I'll see you this evening, okay?"

"See you then."

"I love you, baby."

"I love you, too."

Simone set her phone on her desk and tried to calm her nerves. She knew Chris meant well, but she wished he could somehow understand how important it was for her to network and build a relationship with a published author. And if Simone was truthful with herself, she now knew that she didn't just want to be one of Traci's colleagues, she wanted to be her friend.

Still, whether Chris agreed with her or not, Simone couldn't help thinking how blessed she was to have him in her life. He was a good man with a good heart, and she knew he loved her. She did have her moments of doubt thanks to the disastrous way her last engagement had turned out, but deep down, she believed Chris was honest and sincere about his feelings for her. She'd seen a certain level of decency in his eyes the first day they'd met; and as fate would have it, one morning she'd gone to drop off her car at the dealership to have her brakes replaced, and while she'd been waiting for the serviceman to get her the keys to a loaner, Chris had come in to drop off his SUV. Their attraction for each other had been immediate, but after exchanging a bit of small talk, they'd said their good-byes and gone their separate ways. Then, to Simone's surprise, they'd both ended up returning to pick up their vehicles only minutes apart, and Chris had struck up another conversation with her. Except this time, he'd asked her if it would be okay if he called her. Simone had been hoping she could see him again, and from there, the two of them had connected, become exceptionally close, and gotten engaged. He was the man of her dreams—so caring, so loving, and so genuine.

Still, she couldn't help praying that he wouldn't change. She didn't pray about much, but she certainly prayed regularly for that. She also prayed that Chris would remain loyal to her, and that he wouldn't turn against her the way her last fiancé had; that no matter what happened, good or bad, he would stand up for her and protect her at all costs. What Simone wanted was for him to side with her regardless of the circumstances. She wanted him to take his vows as seriously as she was planning to take hers, and she believed he would. Or again...she prayed he wouldn't change. She hoped he wouldn't disappoint her, because she wasn't a very understanding person—not when people failed to keep their word. She didn't want to be vengeful or unforgiving, she truly didn't. But it was simply who she was, and she couldn't change that.

Chapter 7

Traci revved up the speed of the treadmill, preparing to finish her morning workout. It was a gorgeous, unseasonably warm day in March, and just gazing through the picture window in their lower-level workout room was motivating. It was the reason she'd now been alternating between walking and running for nearly an hour when she normally stopped after about thirty or forty minutes.

She half turned around, though, when she saw Tim walk up behind her.

He stepped up on the side of the treadmill, kissed her on the cheek, and stepped back down. "I'm about to go pick up your dad, but I'll see you later, okay?"

"See you later, baby, and you and Daddy have a great time."

"We will, and I'll call you when I'm headed home to see if you need anything."

"Sounds good."

Tim walked up the stairs, heading out to the church for their monthly men's breakfast, and Traci walked a few minutes longer. But as she prepared to end her cool-down session, the phone rang. She knew it was her mother, Janet, calling so that she, Traci, and Traci's sister, Robin, could have their weekly Saturday-morning conversation.

Traci stopped the treadmill, hopped off of it, and hurried into the family room to answer the phone. "Hi, Mom."

"Hey, sweetheart," Janet said. "How are you this morning?"

"Great. What about you?"

"Couldn't be better."

"Good, and how is Daddy?"

"He's fine. I think he's downstairs waiting for Tim."

"Tim just left a little while ago."

"So what are you up to?" her mom asked.

Traci walked back into the exercise room, picked up her towel, and wiped her face and chest. "I just finished working out."

"Good for you. I've really been slacking this week, but I'm going to get back to it on Monday."

"I didn't feel like doing anything today, either, but now I'm glad I did. I feel a lot more energized."

"I'm sure."

"Oh well, I guess I'd better call up my sis," Traci said, plopping down on the family room's leather sofa.

"Okay, go ahead," Janet said.

Traci loved that she, her mom, and her sister had been doing this for years, sharing a phone call every single week, and sometimes they did it on a weeknight if one of them had special news to share or needed advice on something. The three of them were as close as could be, and Traci cherished their relationship. She also loved how close she was to her twenty-year-old nephew, Ethan, who was a junior at Northwestern University, studying economics and political science.

When the phone rang the first time, Traci connected all three parties.

Robin answered with her usual words: "Good morning, Mommy. Good morning, T."

"Hey, sis," Traci said.

"Good morning, honey," Janet greeted her daughter. "How's it going?"

"Well, I've certainly been better, Mom."

"Really? Why?"

"This new girlfriend of Ethan's is driving me crazy. She's so controlling."

Traci shook her head, laughing.

Janet chuckled, too.

"What?" Robin said. "What's so funny?"

"What's funny is that you're acting like this is some sort of news flash," Traci said, and she and Janet laughed again.

"Please," Robin said in disregard.

"Please nothing," Traci told her. "You've never liked one girl Ethan has dated, not even when he was in high school. There was always something wrong with them or something you just couldn't seem to put your finger on."

"And I was right, too."

"Hmmph," Janet replied. "Not always. Because if I remember correctly, Sasha was as perfect as any of us could have wanted for Ethan. She was beautiful, smart, kind, and respectful, and it was a downright shame how she had to constantly go out of her way, trying to get you to like her."

"Mom, please. That is so not true."

"It is true. Am I right, Traci?"

"Yep. Completely, and Robin knows it."

Robin sighed loudly. "You guys just don't understand."

"Meaning what?" Traci asked.

"What it's like having a highly intelligent son and trying to protect him from these gold diggers. Everyone knows that from the time he was a small boy he's wanted to get a law degree and run for president. And all these greedy young girls know he's headed for success. Not to mention, he's very handsome."

"Not everyone is a gold digger, Robin," her mother told her.

"Maybe not, but this *new* young thing is. I can just feel it."

"Why? Isn't she in college as well?" Traci asked.

"Yeah."

"And what is she majoring in? Or have you even asked her?"

"I don't know, but I think she said something about going to law school just like Ethan."

"Really?" Traci said. "Well then, it doesn't sound like she'll need Ethan's money or anyone else's."

"No, I doubt she will," Janet chimed in. "Especially since Ethan just told me the other day that she got a perfect score on her ACT and was offered full academic scholarships at five different schools. She's a super-smart girl, and she sounds very nice to me."

"You know what, Mom," Robin said, sounding irritated, "you had two daughters, and Traci, you didn't want kids at all, so I'm telling you...it's different when you have a son. There's no way either of you can possibly understand, so let's just talk about something else."

Traci shook her head again, because some things never

changed. Traci loved her sister, and she hated that Robin's ex-husband had walked out on her and Ethan when Ethan had only been five. Because had he stayed, there might have been a chance that Robin wouldn't feel as though Ethan was all she had. It wasn't so much that she personally didn't like the girls Ethan had dated in the past or the young woman he was seeing now, it was just that she was terrified of being alone. She saw any girlfriend of his as a threat to her relationship with Ethan, which couldn't have been further from the truth. Ethan loved, loved, loved his mother, so instead of feeling as though she was losing a son, it would have been much better to accept that she might be gaining an amazing daughter-in-law; which meant that all Traci could hope was that her sister would eventually come to terms with this—more so because Traci had seen this kind of thing with mothers and sons before, and it hadn't turned out well, not for the mothers, anyway. It was so unfortunate, but these mothers she knew of had held on much too tightly; they'd continued to be far too possessive and had treated their sons' girlfriends like enemies. In the end, their sons had pulled as far away from their mothers as possible, being forced to choose their girlfriends or wives instead. This was the last thing Traci wanted to happen to her sister, though, and she prayed it wouldn't.

Traci, her sister, and her mom chatted about everything imaginable until it was almost time for Robin to leave for Marie's.

"I was just there on Thursday," Traci said.

"Oh yeah, that's right."

"And I forgot to tell you and Mom I met a local writer."

"At the hair salon?" her mom asked.

"Yep. It was her first time, and she had an appointment with Renee."

"What has she written?" Robin asked.

"A romance novel. She's not published yet, but she wants to be."

"That's wonderful," Janet said, "because I know you've wanted to have a writer friend living right here in the city."

"I have, and while there are other writers living in Mitchell, most of them write nonfiction or they're men."

"That's true," her mother said. "I hope we get to meet her sometime."

"I hope she's not crazy," Robin said matter-of-factly. "Because we all know how that last author-friend situation of yours turned out. That chick Denise went from being your best friend to being your worst enemy. All because her career wasn't going as well as she wanted it to, or more important, it wasn't going as well as yours. I never liked her, anyway, though. She was way too phony."

Traci stood up. "Yeah, but not everyone is like that."

"No, but *she* definitely was," Robin added.

"She was certainly a different bird," Janet said, "but Traci is right. Not everyone is like that."

"Just be careful, sis. That's all I'm asking."

"I will."

"Okay, then, Mom and T., I need to get going. But I'll see you both at church tomorrow."

Traci walked up the stairs to the main floor. "See you, sis."

"See you later, honey," Janet said.

"Love you both."

"Love you, too," Traci and Janet said.

When Robin hung up, Traci and her mom said their good-byes, too, and ended their conversation. Now Traci walked up to her office and signed on to Facebook. The first thing she saw was a friend request from Simone. Traci slid the mouse across the rubber pad and clicked Confirm and also saw that Simone had emailed her.

Actually, now that Traci thought about it, she hadn't checked her email since sending Simone the agent information yesterday. Normally she checked her email all the time, which was way too much, but because she'd gone to the grocery store, and then she and Tim had gone out to dinner, she'd made a point not to check any more email or text messages for the rest of the day.

But now, she saw a message from Simone.

Hi Traci,

I will never be able to thank you enough for calling your agent and sending me not just one but two names of literary agents! I am so truly grateful, and as promised, I've attached the first three chapters of my manuscript. Also, please don't feel bad about telling me the truth, because I really am open to any critiquing you're willing to give. I want to make sure my story is flowing as well as possible between chapters, that my characters are interesting and relatable, and that I haven't written twice as many words or chapters as I need. My entire manuscript is just under a hundred thousand words, and I know that's kind of high for most contemporary romance novels. But anyway, I'll just

*wait to hear what you think of the first three chapters before
I start cutting or changing anything.*

Thank you again, Traci. ☺
Simone

Traci downloaded the chapters right away and read them. When she finished, she smiled because all three of them were excellent. Both main characters had been interesting from the start, and so was the initial story line, and Traci already loved Simone's writing style. Simone had a gift for telling love stories, and her way with words was unique. So much so that it didn't remind Traci of any other author she'd read, and that in itself was special.

Traci set the pages of the manuscript down and responded to Simone.

Simone!

Wow, I'm not sure what I was expecting, but what a great writer you are! Your work is wonderful, and I enjoyed reading all three chapters. It was as if I was reading a story from an author who has written multiple books, and in this business, that means a lot. With each page, I wanted to keep turning to the next, and writing a page-turning book should be every novelist's goal.

I also don't think you're going to have a problem finding a literary agent to represent you or a publisher to acquire your work. But if for some reason things don't work out with either of the names my agent gave me, I would suggest reading the acknowledgments pages of books that have been written by other contemporary romance writers. Because that way you'll be able to see the names of their agents (if they've thanked them), and you'll know that those particular agents already have experience with selling romance books.

But again, I really enjoyed what I've read thus far, and thank you for asking my opinion.

Talk to you soon!
Traci

Traci hit Enter, but not even five minutes later, her cell phone rang. She'd already locked in Simone's contact information, so her name and number displayed across the screen.

"Hey, Simone."

"Oh my gosh, Traci, you have really made my day. I do apologize for calling you without notice, but after reading your email I couldn't help myself. When your email came through to my phone, I had just gotten in my car, but when I read your words I wanted to cry. I was so worried that what I'd written was awful and that you were going to feel like I was wasting your time."

"Girl, please. Not at all. The excerpt really was as great as I said."

"Thank you. And thank you for reading them so quickly, and again, I'm sorry for calling you out of the blue like this."

"It's fine. Really. No worries. And I'd also like to read the rest, if that's okay."

"Are you kidding? I would love for you to do that. I'll read through my manuscript one more time this weekend and will send it to you early next week."

"Great."

"Thank you again, Traci, and I'll talk to you soon."

"Have a great weekend."

Traci set her phone on her desk. She could tell how excited Simone was, but what Simone didn't know was that Traci was excited herself. Mainly because, as her mom had mentioned earlier, Traci had always wanted to find a local author to be friends with. She had her sister and a couple of other close friends, but she'd also wanted to connect with someone who had a passion for writing and the business of publishing. Plus, she truly liked Simone. She seemed kind and outgoing, and Traci looked forward to chatting with her again and also maybe getting together for lunch or dinner. It would be nice having a writer friend right there in Mitchell who wasn't focused on trying to be in competition with her or trying to criticize or judge her. The whole idea of it was refreshing and a blessing, and Traci was glad to know Simone. She was glad God had allowed their paths to cross.

Chapter 8

As Chris slowed his SUV, waiting for security to direct him down a parking aisle, Simone pulled down the sun visor and looked into the mirror. They were only minutes away from walking inside Deliverance Outreach, where world-renowned reverend Curtis Black was pastor, and she wanted to make sure her makeup was perfect. She also checked her hair for any flyaway strands, but none were out of place.

Chris rolled slowly behind a row of cars and then turned into a parking space on the end. "I still don't understand why you were so adamant about coming here today—a church *I* haven't even been to. As a matter of fact, you've only gone to my church one time, and I practically had to beg you to do that."

Simone stared straight ahead. "But I go there for our marriage counseling."

Chris turned off the ignition and looked at her. "Baby, please don't do that. When I say you don't go to church, you know what I mean. You never go on Sundays or to any actual service."

"I know, but lately I've been thinking a lot more about it. I've actually been thinking about it for a while."

"Yeah, okay," he said, opening the door to get out.

She rested her hand on the side of his arm, hating that she was getting ready to lie to him. "Baby, I'm serious. I know you don't like the fact that I don't go to church, so I've really been praying about it and asking God to give me the desire to go. That's why I've been viewing videos of sermons online, and when I saw one of Reverend Black's it really kept my attention."

"I have no doubt that Pastor Black is a great minister, but I also don't see a reason to leave the church I've been a member of my whole life."

Simone could tell he was becoming upset, so she hurried to pacify him. "I know that, baby, and I don't blame you. So all we're doing is visiting. That's all."

As they made their way through the parking lot toward the church, Simone couldn't help noticing how beautiful Deliverance Outreach was. Then once they strolled inside, she saw that it was even more picturesque and spacious than she'd realized. For some reason, the idea of being there made her excited, which was strange, because with the exception of that one time she'd gone to service with Chris, she hadn't attended church since she was a child, and that was only when one of her grandmother's neighbors had taken her. Of course, there was a pretty important reason why she'd made up her mind to attend Deliverance Outreach today and why she'd likely be visiting from now on: After browsing more and more of Traci's Facebook posts and tweets, Simone had soon discovered that Traci was a very spiritual person who wasn't ashamed to let everyone know that she loved, honored, and trusted God. Traci also tended to quote much of what Pastor Black said on Sunday mornings. So when she'd finished speaking with Traci yesterday and had learned that Traci loved her first three chapters, Simone had known she had a lot to be grateful for. Which was the reason she'd then decided that going to church this morning wasn't a bad idea. It was actually a brilliant one, particularly if it meant she would now have at least one more thing in common with Traci.

Simone and Chris walked through the vestibule area, took a couple of programs from a friendly female greeter, and entered the sanctuary. Then, interestingly enough, as they made their way farther down the aisle and into a row of plush red auditorium-style chairs, Simone spotted Traci, Traci's husband, her mother, her father, and her sister. Simone recognized all of them because of how well she'd studied Traci's photos online. But what were the chances of her sitting so close to Traci and her family—just two rows behind and one section over—when the church easily seated two thousand people? This had to be a sign. What it clearly meant was that Simone was, in fact, supposed to be here today, and she was glad she'd followed her intuition. She was also thrilled that she'd changed her mind about waiting to send the rest of her manuscript to Traci next week, and that she'd spent all of yesterday afternoon and evening proofing it. She'd stayed up until just after midnight so that she could forward it to her new friend as soon as possible.

Simone tried not to stare at Traci and her family, but she couldn't help it—and part of her was hoping that, at some point,

Traci would turn around and notice her. But soon Chris started talking to her, and she had to stop looking in that direction.

Chris made himself more comfortable in his seat and scanned the room. "I'd heard a long time ago how nice the sanctuary was here, but it's just too large for me."

Simone gazed at him for a couple of seconds but didn't say anything. Finally, she returned her attention to Traci, and just as she'd hoped, Traci turned around at that very moment and did a double take. Then she smiled and waved at Simone.

Simone smiled and waved back, and Traci got up and left the row she was sitting in.

"Hey, how are you?" Traci said, hugging her, and now Simone knew Traci truly was as humble as she'd seemed.

"I'm good. And this is Chris, my fiancé," She said, turning toward him. "Chris, this is Traci."

Traci shook his hand. "It's very nice to meet you, Chris."

"It's nice to meet you as well."

"It's really great to see you here," Traci said. "Have either of you attended before?"

Simone shook her head. "No, we haven't."

"I've been a member of Living Faith Ministries since I was a child," Chris added. "But Simone wanted to visit, so here we are."

"Well, it's good having you both, and welcome."

Simone and Chris both said, "Thanks."

Traci looked toward the front of the church. "It looks like praise and worship is about to start, so I'd better get back to my seat. But take care."

"You too," Simone said.

Chris nodded. "It was very nice meeting you."

"It was nice meeting you also."

Simone watched Traci from the time she walked away until the time she slid back into her row and sat down next to her husband.

"Did you know Traci was a member here?" Chris asked.

Simone didn't see why it mattered one way or the other. "No, so how ironic is that?"

Chris looked straight ahead, his tone sarcastic. "It's *very* ironic. Almost too ironic."

"What? You think I'm lying?"

Chris quietly laughed under his breath, and thankfully the organist and musicians began playing their instruments. When praise and worship ended, Pastor Black walked up the steps of the pulpit and stood in front of the glass podium.

"Today is the day the Lord hath made, so let us rejoice and be glad in it."

"Amen," most of the congregation agreed.

"As always, it's great to be in the house of the Lord just one more time," Pastor Black said, and now Simone understood why she'd heard others talk about how charismatic he was. He'd only said a few words and had only been standing before them for a couple of minutes, yet Simone couldn't wait to hear what he had to say next. The way he looked and the way he spoke automatically held your attention.

Simone scanned the sanctuary and didn't see an empty seat. She'd never attended a church this size before, and while Chris didn't care for larger ministries, she didn't see anything wrong with it. Regardless of how big or small a church was, to her, church was church, and she was definitely coming back here again.

"In three weeks, we'll be celebrating Resurrection Sunday, and I really hope all of you are planning to attend our evening Good Friday service. We'll be reflecting on the seven last words of Jesus. By now, most of you know that when we say 'Jesus's seven last words,' we don't mean just seven words, but actually, it's the last seven times he spoke separate sentences. Resurrection Sunday also marks the end of Lent, and I'm sure some of you are already thinking about the dessert, coffee, meat, and sodas you gave up."

Everyone laughed.

Pastor Black laughed, too. "Believe me, I completely understand, but I hope you really are using this time to pray and meditate more than ever before," he said, turning the pages of his Bible. "All right then...so if you would, please turn with me to first Samuel sixteen, seven."

Some members turned the pages of their print Bibles and some tapped their electronic tablets.

"Do we all have it?" Pastor Black asked.

"Yes," most everyone answered.

"Good, and the scripture reads as follows: 'But the Lord said to Samuel, "Don't judge by his appearance or height, for I have rejected him. The Lord doesn't see things the way you see them. People judge by outward appearance, but the Lord looks at the heart."'"

Pastor Black stepped to the side of the podium and said, "So today, I want to speak on the subject Pretending to Be Someone You're Not and the Ultimate Consequences."

Many of the parishioners chuckled and acted as though they could relate to the topic Pastor Black would be speaking on. Simone, of course, had no clue why, because she could never pretend to be something or someone she wasn't. As a matter of fact, if there were people who actually lived their lives that way, she felt sorry for them.

"Have you ever met a person who just doesn't like themselves the way they are? Who can't think for themselves? Who spends most of their days trying to figure out how to be like someone else? Who doesn't feel validated or worthy unless they're doing exactly what another person is doing *and* doing it exactly the way that person does it?"

"Yes," Simone heard many people exclaiming throughout the sanctuary.

"And have you ever met someone who has put on such a noticeable façade for so long that not only do you not recognize who they are anymore, but they don't even recognize who they are themselves? I'm pretty sure you have, and just like all of you, I've met many people like this as well. But I'm here to tell you that trying to be like someone else can only lead to three hundred and sixty-five days of misery, year after year after year. Forgetting about your own likes and dislikes—your own identity—and deciding that someone else's likes and dislikes are better than yours can only lead to daily disappointment. When you stop focusing on your own God-given talents, gifts, and abilities, you will never find true happiness. You will never fully realize your passion, purpose, or the calling that God has on your life. Instead, you will struggle with pain and frustration until the end of time, and the only way to change that is to get back to being you."

Simone sat listening, and while she still thought Pastor Black was a dynamic speaker, she just couldn't relate to what he was preaching about today. So it wasn't long before her attention wandered away, and she glanced over at Traci. She stared at her hair texture and length and decided at that very second that she was getting hair extensions. She was also going to see if she could find that red sheath dress Traci was wearing. It looked so much better than the old-style suit Simone had on. Actually, Simone had just purchased this suit one month ago, but as soon as she walked inside her condo this afternoon, she was stripping it off and dumping it in the trash. What in the world had she been thinking when she'd bought it in the first place? Sheath dresses were so much more classic and fitted, and she was going to buy more of them...just like Traci. And after that, she'd have to find a way to tell Chris that she no longer wanted the two-karat diamond ring he'd proposed to her with. When Simone had met Traci at the salon, she hadn't paid much attention to it, but a few minutes ago she'd seen the double-row diamond wedding band on Traci's finger. Simone loved this idea more than she did wearing a round-cut engagement solitaire and matching gold band, and when the time was right she would tell Chris how she felt about it. She wasn't sure if he'd be upset about it or not, but wearing only a double-row diamond band was what she wanted. It was what she needed...just like Traci.

Chapter 9

When the hostess at Three Rivers Bistro set their menus in front of them and walked away, Simone felt as though she were having an out-of-body experience. Meeting Traci Calloway Cole by chance at a hair salon, getting her to read her novel, and attending the same church with her was already more than Simone could've wished for, but having dinner with her at a popular restaurant was priceless. It was simply unreal, and Simone hoped this wasn't some dream she'd eventually have to wake up from.

But Simone knew it wasn't a dream and now hung her brand-new Gucci handbag across the arm of the chair and got comfortable. As expected, her purse had arrived on Saturday, and she loved it. "Thank you so much for inviting me here."

"I'm glad we could get together," Traci said, looking at the handbag. "Wow, I have that exact same purse. I don't know if you saw it, but I was carrying it when we were at the hair salon."

Simone smiled. "Really? Talk about coincidences and having the same tastes."

"That's for sure. It really is a nice bag, though."

"I know. And, hey, thank you for reading my book. I never imagined that you would get through it so quickly."

"Sunday afternoons are my favorite time to read. So once we left church and went to dinner with my family, Tim and I came home to relax. He turned on the game, and I printed out your manuscript."

"I still can't believe you finished it, though."

"I read most of it yesterday and the rest this morning. It really is that good. Loved it."

"Wow, that certainly encourages and inspires me to keep moving forward."

"I'm glad, because you truly are a great writer. Your book is wonderful."

"I finally found a couple of freelance editors online," Simone said. "So once I hear back from them, I'm going to hire one or the other."

"Good."

Simone actually wasn't planning to do anything of the sort, not when a published writer had already told her how great her work was. But because Traci had suggested that she hire an editor, copyeditor, and proofreader, Simone didn't want her to think she was ignoring her advice. She was planning to hire a proofreader, but that would be it.

Traci sipped some of her water. "So, did you and Chris enjoy service yesterday?"

"We really did. I've always loved going to church, even before I moved here, but I've sort of been looking for another one to join. I go with Chris all the time, but I just feel like I need to be somewhere different."

"Not every church is for every person, but I know you'll

find the right one. Although, how does Chris feel about that? Especially since he's gone to his current church for so many years."

Simone had forgotten about Chris mentioning that to Traci yesterday when he'd met her. "Yeah, he has, but I'm hoping he'll eventually be open to other options."

"I totally understand that, because I'm sure you don't want to attend separate churches."

"No, definitely not. We're getting married next year, and I wouldn't want to join a church that he's not a member of."

"Well, I'll be praying for you to find exactly where the two of you are supposed to be."

"Actually, I really liked Deliverance Outreach. I also enjoyed hearing Pastor Black."

"He's an excellent minister. He doesn't have a perfect history, which I'm sure you know, but a few years ago he became a totally different person. He became a true man of God with real integrity."

"That's amazing."

"He and his family have been through a lot and done a lot, but they're still good people. And no matter what, they've always cared about the church and its congregation and wanted the best for us."

"That's really good to hear, and I look forward to visiting again."

Simone scanned the Venetian-themed restaurant and saw a waitress heading toward them.

"Good evening," the caramel-skinned woman said. "My name is Lezlie, and I'll be taking care of you."

Simone and Traci spoke at the same time. "Good evening."

"I see our hostess has already brought you water, but is there anything else you would like to drink?"

Simone would have loved a glass of wine, but she watched and waited for Traci to answer first.

"No, I'm good," Traci told her.

"Same here," Simone said. "I'm good, too."

"Great. And are you ready to order?"

Traci laughed. "Well, we would be except we've been talking so much, we haven't had a chance to look at the menu. Although, to be honest, I always get the same thing every time I come here. So I'll have your broiled salmon."

Simone had only been there twice before, but each time she'd ordered stuffed shrimp and had loved it.

"What about you?" the waitress asked Simone. "Do you need more time to decide?"

"No, I'd like to have broiled salmon, too. I had it the last time I was here, and it was delicious."

"Okay, then," the woman said. "And would either of you like soup or a salad?"

Traci nodded. "I'll take a side Caesar."

"Me too," Simone added.

"Fine. I'll get everything entered into our system."

"Thanks," Traci said.

Simone drank some of her water. "Oh, and by the way, it was very nice meeting your family yesterday. They all seemed so nice."

"They were glad to meet you as well, and yes, they're the best and beyond supportive. My husband supports my writing career over and above anything I could ever ask for, and so do my parents and my sister. All four of them are my best friends in the world, and I can't imagine having a life without them."

"That's wonderful."

"What about your family? Are you close to your parents?"

"Not really, but only because a few years ago they moved to California and I don't get out there very often. I try to go at least once or twice a year, but sometimes I don't get to."

"I'm really sorry to hear that."

"But don't get me wrong," she hurried to add, "I love my mom and grandmother with all my heart. I grew up with nothing and sometimes I went to bed hungry, but they did the best they could. They're also both very strong, devout Christian women, so even with me growing up on welfare, they were still good role models. They were also very loving and caring."

"The way our parents treat us is the most important thing, anyway. Money and success are great, but our emotional well-being is what really counts. Being loved and cared for helps us to become the best we can be."

"I agree" was all Simone said, knowing that she'd just lied about almost everything. She *had* told the truth about growing up poor, but there was no way she was going to tell Traci that her mother and grandmother lived right there in the Midwest, that her mother was strung out on drugs and her grandmother cursed worse than ten sailors. She certainly wasn't going to admit that she consistently went out of her way to avoid them and never saw them under any circumstances; not when she could already tell how close Traci was with her own family.

"So what do you do at the insurance company you work for?" Traci asked.

"I'm a claims manager," Simone said. This wasn't true, either, but having the title *claims manager* versus *claims specialist* sounded much better to her, and with all the training she sometimes did for incoming employees, she felt as though she had a staff of people reporting to her, anyway.

"Do you like it?"

"For the most part, but my goal is to become a full-time writer."

"I hear you. I remember feeling the same way when I was working my day job. I worked at a bank as a branch manager for years. I loved what I did, but in my heart I knew my passion was writing."

"It's hard not being able to do what you love all the time. I struggle with that every day."

"I can imagine, but it won't always be this way. You'll find an agent and get published, and your book will do very well. And then you'll write and sell your next book or maybe two or more of them at the same time. You just have to hang in there and keep your faith strong."

"I really hope you're right."

"I am. You'll see."

Simone loved how positive Traci was and how she genuinely wanted her to be successful. She had an amazing spirit and noticeable confidence, and she cared about more than just herself.

They chatted until their meals arrived, and when they finished, their waitress brought their bill. Traci pulled out her credit card.

But Simone stopped her. "How much is it?"

"I've got it. My treat."

"Are you sure?"

"Absolutely. I'm just glad we could do this."

"Thank you so much, Traci."

"Anytime," she said, looking at her watch. "Wow, it's earlier than I thought, so I think I'll head across the street to the mall. I need to pick up a couple of makeup items."

"I wouldn't mind browsing around as well if that's okay."

"Of course. Shopping is always a lot more fun when you can do it with a friend."

Simone smiled, but not because Traci was fine with her going to the mall with her. She was excited because Traci had finally said the word *friend*. Simone already considered them to be friends, but now Traci had confirmed that she felt the same way. So life was good.

Actually, it couldn't have been better.

Chapter 10

After Traci purchased the same brand of eyeliner and mascara she'd used for the last ten years, she and Simone moseyed over to the shoe department. They hadn't browsed a full minute before Traci saw a pair of flat rhinestone sandals she loved.

"Aren't these cute?" she said to Simone. "And so unique."

"They really are."

Traci examined them, top, side, and bottom, and then looked at the price. "They're not on sale, but I still think one of my Macy's coupons will work on these."

Simone moved closer to the next table and picked up another pair.

Traci walked toward the checkout counter, where a saleslady was standing. "Hi. Can you check to see if you have these in a ten?"

"Sure," the young woman told her. "I'll be right back."

"Thank you."

Traci walked from table to table, checking out more shoes, but none struck her the way the first pair had. So she hoped the store had them in stock.

A couple of minutes later, the salesgirl returned. "You're in luck. We don't get a lot of tens, and this is our last pair. And even though we just got this style in, they're going pretty fast."

"I can see why," Traci said, sitting down and taking one of the sandals from the box. She slipped it on, buckled it at the side, and did the same with the matching one. She already loved the way they felt, so she walked over to the full-length mirror to see how they looked. She had on a pair of jeans, and the sandals looked amazing. She also wanted to wear them with shorts or capris, so she rolled her pants legs up to her knees and glanced at the mirror again. "I really do love these."

The salesgirl nodded. "So do I."

Simone walked over and folded her arms. "They're definitely cute and very different."

Traci sat down to take them off and told the salesgirl, "I'll take them."

"Wonderful."

Traci removed both sandals, placed them back in the box, and gave them to the young lady to ring up. Then, after she paid for them with her Macy's card, she and Simone headed toward the jewelry section.

Simone went around to the left side of the counter, and Traci stopped at the front of it and pulled a pair of sterling silver hoops from the display. She loved hoops for daily wear and large, bold earrings for dressier outfits, but these could be worn for any occasion. They were dressy and casual all in one, so she held on to them. She also looked at a few more earrings and bracelets, but when she didn't see anything else she wanted, she gave the hoops to the fiftysomething woman behind the counter.

"Will that be all?" the woman said.

"I think so."

The woman scanned the bar code on the back of the plastic board the earrings were attached to and then set them on white tissue paper, preparing to wrap them. "If you'll swipe your Macy's card, any reward coupons you have will appear on-screen."

Traci slid her card through the machine, clicked on one of the coupons just as she had in the shoe department, and waited for her total. Then she signed her name and hit Enter.

The saleslady packaged up the earrings. "Would you like your receipt with you or in the bag?"

Traci reached her hand out. "I'll take it."

"Here you are, and please enjoy."

"I will, and thank you."

Simone had been standing behind Traci, not saying anything, but now Traci realized she was waiting to pay for something.

"What did you find?" Traci asked.

"Just a pair of pearl earrings," she said, showing them to Traci.

"Those are pretty. I love pearls."

Simone passed the earrings to the saleslady. "I do, too."

When Simone had completed her transaction, Traci said, "You want to head upstairs to the clothing department?"

"Sounds good to me," Simone told her, and they went over to the escalator and got on.

As they rode up to the second floor, Traci looked back

across the first level. "The sales are never that great on a Monday, but I sort of like shopping when there's hardly anyone in the store."

"Me too," Simone said. "It's a lot easier to look for what you want, and you don't have to wait to try anything on or pay for it."

Traci stepped off the escalator. "Exactly."

Simone got off next. "I think I'll head to the dress area."

"Okay. I'll be over there," Traci said, pointing to tops and blouses, but then she heard her phone ring. "Hey, sweetheart," she said to her husband.

"Hey, baby. Where are you?"

"At the mall."

"How was dinner?"

"We had a great time, and actually, Simone is here at the mall, too."

"Wow, you really do like her, don't you?"

"I do. She's a good person."

"And she's a writer," he said.

"Yep, and I need that. Because when you're self-employed, it's not like you have coworkers that you can see every day or do things with."

"I hear you, and I agree, but I just hope she doesn't end up being like that last author you thought was your friend."

Traci pulled a sleeveless white knit top from the rack. "Don't even remind me. Although Robin just talked about that very thing on Saturday."

"That's because we all saw what a disaster it was. But I always told you that something wasn't right with her, and that you needed to be careful."

"I know, but Denise has betrayed every author she's ever come in contact with, and I don't think Simone is like that."

"Maybe not, but it's not like you really know her."

"No, but with the exception of Denise, I've always been a pretty good judge of character. I can tell when people genuinely don't like me, and when they're trying to hurt me in some way. Plus, I'm the one who asked Simone out to dinner."

"Yeah, but she emailed you the same day she met you, right? And then she showed up at church yesterday."

Traci couldn't deny that this seemed like too much of a coincidence, but she didn't think it was a big deal. "I agree, but at the same time, a lot of people visit our church just because of Pastor Black and how well-known he is."

"Okay, but I'm going to say what I always say: Please be careful."

"I will."

"So how much longer are you going to be?"

"Not long," she said, now picking up the same sleeveless top she was already holding, except this one was black. "I'm going to pay for a couple of items I just found, and then I'll be home."

"Good, because you know I'm waiting for you, right?"

"Yeah, I bet. That's the real reason you called me in the first place."

"Yep, and I'm not ashamed of it, either," he said, laughing.

Traci laughed, too. "You crack me up."

"Okay, let me get back to my game. But I'll see you soon."

"All right. Love you."

"Love you, too, baby."

Traci ended the call and dropped her phone in her purse. Fifteen years had passed, yet there were times when Traci felt like she and Tim were still on their honeymoon. They'd had arguments and problems like any other couple, but the one thing she knew for sure was that they were meant to be together. Tim was a kind, loving, supportive man who kept God first and her second, no matter what happened. He was good *to* her and good *for* her, and she loved him with everything inside of her. He also worried a lot about her well-being, and even more so when he thought she might be setting herself up for pain and disappointment. She knew he was right in all that he'd said, but she couldn't help the way she felt; how she had this great desire to help and advise people.

More than anything, she wanted to prevent others from making some of the past mistakes she'd made. So when she met young women who were in verbally or physically abusive relationships, she shared everything she could with them about her first marriage and tried to be there for them. Then, when she met aspiring writers who were talented and serious about making it in publishing, she tried to tell them all that she could when it came to what might work and what might not work for them. Mostly because when she'd finished writing her first book, she'd made a few blunders, which probably could have been avoided had she been able to find a knowledgeable mentor. The same went for relationships—as in, had she been close to a woman who'd gotten into and out of a terrible marriage, she wouldn't have become so easily involved with her first husband. So now that Traci had overcome her obstacles—her first marriage and having her first book rejected multiple times—she felt an obligation to help others when she could. She wasn't a pushover, not by any stretch of the imagination, but she did believe in giving most people a chance to prove themselves. Plus, there was something sad about Simone's demeanor. She smiled enough, talked enough, and was nice enough, but in some ways, she seemed lonely and unhappy. Traci had specifically noticed it when she talked about how poor she'd been as a child, even though Simone had tried to keep a joyful face. It was just something about the look in her eyes, almost as if her childhood had been much worse than she'd mentioned to Traci, and that Simone needed validation for anything she said or did. It wasn't a problem for Traci, but one of the things she had noticed was the way Simone had waited to order her food. Traci had even seen her looking at her as though she hadn't wanted to make any selections until then. It may have seemed crazy for Traci to suspect this, but it was just a feeling she had. Lots of people only drank water when they went out to dinner, many ordered a side Caesar as their salad, and countless people loved eating salmon. However, it just seemed that Simone would've ordered anything that Traci had ordered, regardless of what it was.

Still, Traci liked Simone, and she was going to help her with getting published. Then, once that happened, she would recommend Simone's work to her own readers. She would do what she wished someone had been willing to do for her.

Simone drove around the outskirts of the entire mall twice, until she was sure Traci had left the parking lot. Not long ago, they'd walked outside, said their good-byes, and prepared to head home, but Simone had come up with a different plan, which was the reason she reparked her car, walked back inside Macy's, and headed straight to the shoe department.

She went over to the first table that Traci had stopped at earlier and picked up the sandals that the two of them had loved so much.

The same salesgirl walked up to her. "Can I get something for you?"

"Yes, do you have these in a nine?"

"I think I saw a couple of them when I went to look for your friend, but let me check."

Simone took a seat and hoped the woman was right. As it was, when she'd told Traci that she'd given her the last size ten, Simone had worried that they might not have her size at all. Although, if they didn't, Simone would just order them online.

She waited for a few minutes and smiled when the woman came out with a box in her hand.

"Here you go, and interestingly enough, we didn't have two nines like I'd thought. We only have this one, so I guess it was meant for you."

"I guess so," Simone said, slipping off her kitten-heel ankle boots. Thankfully, she hadn't worn any tights or knee-highs, which made it easy to try on the sandals.

"Those look great on you," the salesgirl said.

"I really love these. I've seen a lot of rhinestone sandals, but these are in a category all by themselves."

"That they are. So I take it you want them?"

"I do."

Simone pulled them off and handed them to the woman.

"Will this be on your Macy's card?" she asked.

"Uh, I don't have one, but I'll still be using a credit card."

"You do know that if you open an account now, you'll get a twenty percent discount."

Simone debated it, but because she already had an American Express card, two Visas, and two MasterCards, she'd made a pact a long time ago not to open very many department store cards. She did have one from Nordstrom, but that was a Nordstrom Visa. So, technically, she actually had three Visas and her only department store cards were from Victoria's Secret and Target. But nonetheless, if Traci had a Macy's card it was likely worth her getting one of those, too. So Simone debated her decision again and again. She did want one, but if there was one thing she was proud of it was the fact that she had excellent credit. This hadn't always been the case, but since filing for bankruptcy ten years ago, she'd changed the way she handled using credit cards. Every now and then, she tended to buy things she didn't need, but entering bankruptcy had taught her a very valuable and humiliating lesson, and she never wanted to live like that again. She also didn't want to take a chance on struggling and living in poverty the way she had as a child. So once her bankruptcy had been wiped from her credit report three years ago, she'd slowly but surely begun building her credit back up and now she had six major credit cards to show for it.

"No," Simone said, "I think I'll pass."

"Okay, but if you change your mind, you can apply at any time."

After Simone paid for her shoes, she left and went over to the jewelry counter. Before doing anything else, she grabbed the same pair of sterling silver hoops that Traci had purchased.

"So you're back," the fiftysomething woman said.

"Yes, I decided I don't want the pearl earrings. I'd like to exchange them for these."

"No problem," she said. "Actually, I hadn't seen these until your friend picked them up to look at them."

Simone didn't say anything, but for some reason she thought about Traci and how she'd said she loved pearls. So maybe she should keep them after all. Should she or shouldn't she? Because it wasn't like Simone wore pearls all that much. She also wasn't sure she liked this particular pair as much as she'd thought she had.

She debated the pearl earrings again and then ultimately decided against them. Still, she had one more department to return to, so she went upstairs to women's clothing. When Traci had answered her husband's call, not only had Simone seen her talking to him at a distance, but she'd also seen her pick up two classy sleeveless summer sweaters. The material was very thin, but they were perfect for jeans, dress pants, or even a skirt. Normally Simone didn't wear a lot of sleeveless clothing, but after seeing Traci in her red sheath dress yesterday and then seeing her buy the two tops tonight, she realized how much she actually did like this sort of style.

So she pulled a white and a black one from the rack and carried them over to the checkout counter.

"How are you?" the saleslady said.

"I'm fine, and you?"

"Wonderful, now that I only have another hour to work."

Simone smiled.

"Will this be all?"

"Yes."

The woman removed both tops from their hangers. "These are the same two that your friend just bought, right?"

"Um, yes. We like a lot of the same clothing, so this happens pretty often."

"Then you must have to call each other all the time. You know, whenever you're going somewhere together," the woman said, laughing.

Simone half smiled, because she didn't see what was so funny. Simone and Traci simply had similar tastes, and there was nothing wrong with that. Simone hadn't seen one item that Traci had worn in person or in her photos that she didn't like, so this was proof that they loved the same things. They had similar opinions, the same eye for clothing and shoes, and they both had a passion for writing and storytelling. It was as if they'd known each other for years—as if they'd been best friends for decades—and Simone was happy that everything was going so well between them. She did have a couple of friends who were more like acquaintances, but she didn't have any ride-or-die friends so to speak. It wasn't because she didn't want any, it was just that the few friends she currently had, and even those from her past, didn't understand her. But none of that mattered to her anymore, not when she could tell how loyal Traci was and that she was a real friend. Not when Simone believed wholeheartedly that Traci would be her best friend from now on.

Chapter 11

Simone set all her new items on her bed and went into her office. She'd just arrived home, but during her drive, all she'd been able to think about was the red sheath dress she'd seen Traci wearing at church yesterday. She hadn't been able to take her mind off of it, and she knew it was because it was the perfect dress for her. It was the kind of dress she could wear to church or work, and she had to have it.

She signed on to her computer and went to Macy's web site. She searched and searched again, but she didn't see the dress Traci had worn. Finally she perused Lord & Taylor's site, and then Dillard's, and then those for Saks Fifth Avenue, White House Black Market, Ann Taylor, and Talbots.

"Where is it?" she said out loud. "I know one of these stores has to have it."

Simone sighed heavily and started over again. It was then that she realized she'd searched for "red sheath dress" and not "sleeveless red sheath dress." So now she browsed the Macy's site with the correct keywords, and then she moved on to Nordstrom's. She scrolled down the first page and also the second and third, and suddenly she found what looked to be the exact same dress...but then when she enlarged the graphic of the model who was wearing it, she noticed that the stitching around the collar and toward the waist were different.

She sighed with more intensity than before. Where had Traci gotten that dress from? Although, what if she'd purchased it a long time ago, and it was no longer available?

Still, Simone wasn't about to give up. Not until she'd exhausted all options, and it was a good thing she hadn't because when she pulled up the Talbots page again, she found precisely what she'd been looking for. She wasn't sure how she'd missed it the first time, but here it was displayed on her screen. Finally. She couldn't have felt more relieved, and she hurried to order it before something crazy happened, such as the dress being backordered or, heaven forbid, they ended up not having her size. But thankfully, they did have her size, so she placed her order and moved on to her next to-do item: looking for the shoes she'd seen Traci wearing with the red dress. Black patent-leather pointed-toe pumps. They'd had noticeable detail, too, mainly the small lamb leather patch that covered the very tip of the toe area. Simone didn't own a pair of patent-leather shoes, but when she'd seen Traci wearing some yesterday, she'd realized how much she loved and wanted them.

So now she searched Nordstrom again, and lo and behold, she found them in a matter of minutes. She hadn't used her Nordstrom Visa in a while, and she certainly wasn't accustomed to buying shoes that cost two hundred dollars, but these pumps were worth every cent.

Simone typed in her information, but just as she finished her online transaction, her phone rang. She leaned over to see who it was and cringed. It was her grandmother calling. Simone's first thought was to ignore it, but she knew if she did, her grandmother would keep calling day and night, multiple times, until she got in touch with her.

Simone lifted her phone from her desk and accepted the call. "Hello?"

"I'm surprised you even answered," her grandmother exclaimed. "Normally I have to call you ten times 'fo you finally decide to pick up. This from a child I took in, wiped her behind, and raised up like she was my own. Something I didn't have to do."

Simone sat, holding her phone in silence.

"So I guess you don't have nothin' to say. Actually, it don't matter none to me, anyway, because I'm only callin' to letcha know that mama of yours is back strung out on them drugs again. Just a shame how high she was when she stopped by here an hour ago. Wantin' money. I told her she must be out her idiot mind if she thank I'm gone give her one red nickel. But I did tell her I would call to see if *you* wanna send her a little somethin'. I first told her to call you herself, but she said you haven't answered not one of her calls since she talked to you at Christmastime. Is that true?"

"Yep."

"What a flat-out disgrace. Not talking to your own mama. But like I said, she need a little money…and I need a few dollars, too."

"I don't have it," Simone said matter-of-factly.

"You still got that high-payin' job at that insurance company, don't you? Don't you even have fifty dollars you could wire her? And a couple a hundred for me?"

"No. I don't."

"You such a liar and still as uppity as ever. But that's okay, because you know what they say. Every dog has his day. Especially those who run around with big secrets. The kind certain folks wouldn't want their friends in a new city to find out about."

A chill ripped through Simone's body, but she didn't respond.

And this time neither did Velma, who finally hung up on her.

Simone set the phone down and took a deep breath, trying to slow her pulse rate. Her heart was beating much too hard and fast. She wasn't sure why she didn't just get her number changed. That way she wouldn't have to hear from her mother or grandmother again, but there was a part of her that didn't want to cut her grandmother off for good; not when Velma had in fact raised her up just the way she'd said. Still, Simone was ashamed of both her mother and grandmother and wished they'd stop calling her. She wished they'd pretend she didn't exist—she wished her grandmother would stop reminding her about things that had happened in the past. Bad things that most people wouldn't understand. This was exactly the reason she'd never told either of them about Chris or that she was engaged to be married—it was the reason she'd told Chris that her grandmother was the one who didn't want anything to do with her and that she also hadn't spoken to her mother in a couple of years. This was a totally different story from what she'd shared with Traci, but the version she'd given Chris had stopped him from asking when he would be able to meet them—something she could never allow. It was just best to keep them away from him, otherwise they would embarrass her and ruin everything. Life as she knew it would be over, and she would rather die than have that happen.

Chapter 12

Traci leaned over and kissed Tim on the lips, and he held her close. It was six a.m. and time for them to get up, but for some reason, neither of them felt like moving.

"This is one of those days when I wish I could sleep in," he said.

Traci nestled her head closer against his body. "I know. I was thinking the same thing. But," she said, sighing and sitting up, "duty calls."

Tim raised up as well. "That it does."

"Your weekly staff meetings are on Tuesdays, anyway, right?"

"Yep, at nine o'clock. So I really need to get going."

Traci smiled at him. "I am so, so proud of you, baby. I know I keep saying that, but I can't help it. You've worked so hard for so many years, and now you're seeing all the rewards."

"Sometimes I still can't believe it, but I'm truly grateful. I'd always hoped to make it to executive status, but to be honest, I'm not sure I really thought it would happen."

"Well, it did, and you deserve it."

Tim swung his legs toward the floor. "I just wish my parents were here to see that none of their love and support was in vain. I still think about how they paid for all my college expenses so that I wouldn't have to take out any student loans. They went without a lot and never complained."

"You were their only child, and they wanted the best for you. They were such wonderful people."

"They loved you, too...for the little time they got to spend with you. Hard to believe they both passed away in their fifties."

Traci propped her knees on the bed and moved behind Tim. She wrapped her arms around him, resting her cheek against his. "I know. It doesn't seem real, but you couldn't have asked for better parents, and I couldn't have asked for better in-laws."

Tim let out a deep breath, and Traci knew he was having a sad moment. His parents had, in fact, been the best parents any child could have hoped for, but they'd both become ill. Tim's mom had suffered a fatal stroke, and his dad had died from a massive heart attack. Worse, his dad had passed less than a year after his mom, and Tim and Traci both sometimes wondered if he'd died from a broken heart. Especially since he was one of the healthiest men they'd known, and because he'd never been the same emotionally after losing his wife.

"Okay, enough of that," he said, caressing the other side of Traci's face, and although Traci couldn't see his eyes, she was sure they were full of tears.

"Your parents are with you in your heart. Always. And don't you ever forget that."

"I know that, and I love you for being the devoted wife you are. For pushing me to be the best I can be."

"I love you, too, for doing the exact same thing for me.

Without you, I wouldn't have kept trying to get published, but more than anything, I wouldn't have the kind of marriage I'd always hoped for. The kind I'd prayed for."

"The kind we *both* prayed for," he said, turning and kissing her.

They held each other for a while longer but finally went into the bathroom. Tim jumped into the shower, and Traci stood at her vanity, washing her face with cold water the way she did every morning. Then she joined Tim so she could soap and cleanse his back the way he liked.

When Tim got out of the shower and dried off, Traci stayed in a few more minutes with her eyes closed, enjoying the hot steam. She also played through her mind more of the synopsis she was writing for her fourth book. She didn't have much more to add, but she knew something was still missing. She had no idea how the story would end, just like she hadn't with her first three books, but she knew that at least one other plot twist was needed.

So she stood, thinking and rethinking, plotting and replotting until Tim came back into the bathroom.

"You're still showering?"

Traci opened her eyes and gazed through the glass at him. "You're already dressed?"

"Just about. You must be in very deep thought."

"I was, and I guess I lost track of time. Just trying to figure out more of my story."

Tim shook his head, smiling.

"What?" she said.

"Nothing. It's just good to see you doing something you love."

Traci turned off the shower and grabbed her towel. "It really makes a difference."

Tim turned toward the mirror above his vanity, tying his tie, and Traci stepped out.

"Oh well, I guess I'd better get out of here," he said. "Gotta stop at Starbucks on the way."

"Don't I know it. But it's like I always tell you, it would be faster just to make some with the Keurig."

"Yeah, and it's like I always tell you, I need something a lot stronger than that."

"Coffee head," she said.

"That would be me," he said, and kissed her good-bye.

"Have a good day."

"You too, and I'll call you later."

After Traci rubbed her body down with shea butter and threw on a T-shirt and workout pants, she made herself a cup of coffee and went into her office. She was planning to hop on the treadmill but wanted to check her email first. Interestingly enough, though, when she scanned her new messages, she saw multiple notifications that included Simone's first and last name in the subject line. Traci had already accepted Simone's friend request on Facebook, and she'd also seen where Simone had liked a few of her status updates on her public Facebook page, but now she was following Traci on Twitter. And Instagram. And Goodreads. And Periscope. And Google+.

Traci didn't think this was completely unusual, because in many cases, when a person followed you on one form of social media, they tended to follow you on others. This routine was even more likely if the person was highly social media–savvy and spent lots of time on the various platforms daily. Still, for some reason, Traci thought about Tim and what he'd said to her on the phone yesterday when she was shopping: "Please be careful." Tim had his concerns, but even though Traci could see that all the notifications had come through late last night, she decided that the only reason Simone likely wanted to stay so connected was because of her strong desire to get published and have a full-time writing career.

Traci signed on to Facebook to read comments from her readers, but first she searched for Simone's page. When it displayed, Traci checked for photos, but not only did she not see any of Simone's family members or friends, she also didn't see any of her and Chris. Although, not everyone uploaded traditional photos or selfies or wrote comments relating to their personal lives, and Traci didn't blame them. But next, Traci pulled up Simone's Twitter and Instagram pages, and while she had posted graphics of popular sayings and typed some scriptures, she hadn't posted any personal photos through those mediums, either. This did seem a little odd for someone who was registered on so many types of social media, but again, Traci knew not everyone shared in the same manner.

Traci signed off of her computer and went into their workout room. When she stepped onto the treadmill and set the time and incline, she picked up the TV remote and turned it on. She switched it to one of the morning shows and saw a debut *New York Times*–bestselling author being interviewed. Traci didn't think about this a lot, and she rarely compared herself to anyone else, but at this very second, she wondered if her career would ever rise to the level of the young woman she was watching. So far, she'd made a couple of online bookstore bestsellers lists and also some that were compiled by various literary web sites—

which she couldn't be more grateful for—but she hadn't made what most folks in the publishing industry considered to be the top three: the *New York Times*, *USA Today*, and *Publishers Weekly*.

"I'm still in total awe," the young woman said. "As a new author, it was a shock to make the list at all. But to make it the very first week my book went on sale has been a dream."

"How exciting," one of the two female hosts said, "and it sounds like your publisher knew early on just how popular your book was going to be. It's been reported that your advance was one million dollars."

The author smiled and chuckled a bit but didn't comment one way or the other.

The male host smiled, too. "We also hear that they spent the same amount to market and advertise it. Is that true?"

The young woman kept on smiling. "All I'll say is that they really believed in me, and I am completely indebted to them."

"Why do you think your book has been so successful," the second female host asked, "and that it happened so quickly?"

"To put it plainly, it centers on lots and lots of sex with no sugarcoating, and whether we're talking about books, movies, or the Internet, well...sex sells."

The male host chimed in. "So what you've written isn't necessarily what we would call romance."

"No, it's probably more like erotica. Maybe even more intense than that."

Traci wasn't surprised by any of what she was hearing, because for weeks now, she'd been seeing frequent online promotions for the book, national TV commercials had aired, and a massive number of literary blogs had featured it. Traci also knew something else. There were books for all kinds of readers, and there were readers who loved all kinds of books, but if writing graphic, near-porn sex was what it would take for her to sell millions and millions of books, she could forget about ever making it to the top of any national list. For one thing, she wasn't that great at writing even the most tasteful of sex scenes, but more important, this wasn't who she wanted to be as a writer and it didn't represent her Christian and moral values.

Actually, this was part of the reason she loved Simone's novel. It did include sex, but more than anything, the story centered on emotional intimacy, and it showed how in love the hero and heroine were with each other. It painted their beautiful romance in a positive and uplifting light, and there was nothing offensive about it. It showed true chemistry in a relationship and how everyone has a soul mate.

Traci truly did admire what Simone's book represented, and it was the reason that when she finished her workout, she went back into her office. New York was an hour ahead of Mitchell, so Traci picked up her phone and dialed her editor's number. Helen, her agent, had already recommended two great representatives for Simone to contact, but now Traci wanted to take things a step further. She was going to ask her editor, who published both romance and women's fiction, if she would be willing to read Simone's manuscript herself. Traci knew there were no guarantees and that she didn't want Simone getting her hopes up for nothing, so for now, she wouldn't tell her anything about this. But if her editor agreed, Traci would hope and pray for the best. If things worked out, her editor would make an offer, and Simone would be on her way to getting published. She would see her dream become a reality, and that made Traci smile.

Chapter 13

S imone deepened her voice, trying to sound as though she were so ill that she needed to visit the emergency room. "It started last night," she whispered to her boss in a groggy tone, "but I really thought I'd be much better this morning."

"It's not a problem," Roger said. "You just take good care of yourself."

Now she half moaned for full effect. "Thank you so much for understanding. I'm sure it's just some sort of stomach flu, and it shouldn't last too long."

"I hope you feel better soon, and no worries."

"Thank you, Roger."

Simone hung up the phone and set it on her desk. She was sorry about lying to him, but last night she'd written and rewritten her query letter so many times, she'd begun seeing tiny black dots popping across her computer screen. Even now, she'd been up since five a.m., doing the same thing all over again. She was pretty sure the letter was fine, based on the dozens of samples she'd read online, but before she sent this on to Traci, she wanted it to be perfect. So she read the draft yet again, and did more minor editing.

There was one thing she didn't understand, though. Both the literary agents Traci had given her the names of didn't accept query letters longer than one page, and they only accepted the first five pages of the actual manuscript. To Simone, these criteria didn't nearly allow a writer to fully explain her story or introduce herself as a person. Then, as far as the manuscript, how in the world could an agent or anyone else know whether a book was good or not without reading at least a full chapter? Simone knew both requirements were fairly standard, though, because she'd seen the web sites for a number of other agents who had similar guidelines. This was also the reason she had found herself spending hours writing her query letter, trying to figure out a way to trim it down.

Simone made a few more tweaks and then closed out of her Word software and went to Traci's Facebook page. She read the five reader comments that had already been posted this morning and then pulled up Traci's Twitter feed. The first thing she saw was Traci's tweet from two hours ago. It quoted the scripture Philippians 4:13, and read, "'I can do all things through Christ which strengtheneth me.' ~ (KJV)."

It wasn't until now that Simone realized she hadn't posted her own morning scripture, and she had to get better with remembering to do that. She needed to stay consistent—the same as Traci. She wasn't sure what scripture to post, so she Googled "a great motivational scripture." Then, when a number of web sites displayed, she clicked on the second one and saw John 6:47 from the King James Version: "Verily, verily, I say unto you, He that believeth on me hath everlasting life."

She wasn't sure why, but there was something about that particular scripture that she liked. Maybe because it offered a certain sense of hope. But then she saw another verse that talked about strength the same as the scripture Traci's post had mentioned, so she typed that one instead, Isaiah 41:10: "Fear thou not; for I am with thee: be not dismayed; for I am thy God: I will strengthen thee; yea, I will help thee; yea, I will uphold thee with the right hand of my righteousness."

Simone read what she'd typed but then went back to the site where she'd copied the scripture. She actually liked the New Living Translation interpretation better: "Don't be afraid, for I am with you. Don't be discouraged, for I am your God. I will strengthen you and help you. I will hold you up with my victorious right hand." But since Traci always seemed to use the King James Version, Simone would stick with using that. Actually, the more she scrolled through other scriptures, she preferred reading those via the New Living Translation, too, because when she did, the words were much clearer.

Simone browsed Twitter for a few more minutes and then typed in the URL for Traci's web site. When her home page appeared, Simone clicked on the "Media" link and then played a YouTube video of a television interview Traci had done with a Chicago news station last year. It was during the release week for her second book. Simone watched the four-minute segment. Then she watched it again. Then she watched it again. And again. And again. But now she replayed the intro.

"Thank you so much for having me, Donna," Traci said, smiling.

Simone paused the video. "Thank you so much for having me, Donna. Thank you so much for having me, Donna."

Simone played Traci's response again.

"Thank you so much for having me, Donna."

Simone paused the video again. "Thank you so much for having me, Donna," she said, but this time she could tell her tone and diction sounded much more like Traci's than they had the last time. She also smiled and gave two fast nods, exactly the way Traci had.

Simone played the video many more times, all while practicing Traci's words and facial expressions. She also clasped her hands together and rested them in her lap...the same as Traci had.

Soon Simone moved on to every individual response that Traci had given, still practicing and mimicking every aspect of what she saw and heard. Simone started and stopped the video until she had Traci's behavior and enunciation down pat. Then she picked up her smartphone and hit the Record icon.

"Thank you so much for having me, Donna. Thank you so much for having me, Donna."

She stopped the recording and played it back. Then she played this particular part of Traci's YouTube video again. Then she played her phone recording. Then she played the YouTube video again. And then her phone recording. She was so happy with how close her voice sounded to Traci's that her heart beat faster than normal. She was elated because when it came time for her to do TV interviews, she'd be well prepared. Although, there was one thing that bothered her, and that was her name. Traci Calloway Cole had a special ring to it, and sounded a million times better than Simone Phillips. This also made Simone want to forget about planning a wedding, so that she and Chris could get married right away at the courthouse. If they did, she'd be able to use her maiden name and new surname as soon as possible.

"Simone Phillips McCann," she spoke out loud. "Traci Calloway Cole. Simone Phillips McCann. Traci Calloway Cole."

Her future married name sounded okay, she guessed, but if only Chris's last name could start with *Ph* the same as hers, it would be perfect.

She played around with a few examples that would work much better than McCann. "Simone Phillips Phalen. Simone Phillips Phifer."

She would even settle for a last name that began with *F*, since it would still create the precise kind of alliteration she was looking for.

"Simone Phillips Foster," she said. "Simone Phillips Faulkner. Simone Phillips Freeman."

Simone knew there was nothing she could do about Chris's name, but there was a way to fix this little dilemma. She would use a pen name for her books. Writers did this all the time, so why shouldn't she?

She spoke out loud again. "Traci Calloway Cole. Simone Phillips Freeman. Traci Calloway Cole. Simone Phillips Freeman."

Simone smiled as she repeated Traci's name with her new name, over and over and over. It was priceless, and she couldn't wait to use it on her first book, social media pages, and future web site.

But now, Simone got up and walked down the hallway to her bathroom. The whole maiden-name/married-name scenario had forced her attention in a different direction, but it was time she got back to practicing Traci's interview responses.

She stepped in front of the mirror. "Thank you so much for having me, Donna. Thank you so much for having me, Donna. Thank you so much for having me, Donna."

Simone smiled and nodded twice each time, and although she could tell she definitely sounded like Traci and now moved her hands and head in the right way, something was off. Something was missing, and Simone knew what it was.

So she went back down the hallway into her office and sat back down. Then she Googled the phone number for a stylist named Andrea who specialized in hair extensions, the one Simone had heard a coworker talking about. Actually, Simone had seen Andrea's work, and although she'd never cared much for weave, she'd thought it was one of the best undetectable jobs she'd encountered.

Simone dialed the salon.

"Good morning, Andrea's Hair Studio, this is Vivian speaking," a woman said.

"Hi, I'm looking to schedule an appointment."

"Okay, I can help you with that. Do you have an idea of what you'd like to have done?"

"Yes, I'd like to get individual hair extensions."

"Then what I'd first need to do is schedule a consultation for you."

"I work with one of Andrea's clients, so I already know her work. I also know what length and style I want."

"Do you have a photo of it?"

"I do," Simone said, clicking on Traci's author photo on her web site and downloading it.

"Great. Well, if you can email over a copy along with a head shot of yourself, Andrea can take a look. I'll then call you with her price. You can also ask any other questions you might have."

"Sounds good."

The receptionist recited the salon's email address.

"How soon do you think it'll be?"

"Before Andrea can look at your photos?"

"Yes, and also how long it will take to get in."

"Andrea's with a client right now, but she'll probably take a look when she finishes. Then, as far as her calendar goes, she's booked pretty solid until the end of next week."

Simone had been hoping to get in sooner—like tomorrow, if she could—and wondered if she should try a couple of other places. But because she'd heard too many great things about Andrea from her coworker, next week would simply have to do.

"Okay, thanks, and I'll send the photos over shortly."

"I'll be looking for them."

When Simone ended the call, she downloaded the head shot she'd taken of herself to use on social media. Then she typed a short email, attached both photos, and sent it to the receptionist. She was so excited about getting her hair done, and she couldn't wait to hear back from Andrea. Based on Simone's coworker's comments, she knew Andrea didn't come cheap, but Simone didn't care what her hairdo was going to cost. She loved the way Traci wore her thick tresses down on her shoulders, and as far as Simone was concerned, this was an investment. She'd written a book, but once she got it published she'd need to begin promoting it; which meant she needed to look as good as possible. She needed to do what was obviously working for Traci...including dyeing her natural coal-black hair so that it was medium brown...

Just like Traci's.

Chapter 14

*J*raci leaned back in her chair and read the query letter Simone had emailed her this afternoon. Then she read it again, marking a couple of items with a red pen. But overall, the letter sounded fine.

Traci glanced at her watch and saw that it was almost six o'clock, so she dialed Simone's number.

"Hey, Traci," she answered.

"Hey, how are you?"

"Good."

"I know you probably just got home from work, so I can call you back later if you want."

"Uh, no...It's fine...I, uh, got off a little early today."

Traci wondered why Simone was stumbling over her words, but she didn't question her. "Oh, okay, well, if you have a minute we can go over your letter."

"Of course. What did you think?"

"I thought it was great. I wouldn't change anything you've written, and the only items I marked up were a couple of echoes."

"Can you give me an example?"

97

"Yes, and I'll also scan the document and email it to you. But in your second paragraph you used the word 'portray' twice in two consecutive sentences, and in the last paragraph, you ended two consecutive sentences with 'to you.'"

"Thank you for taking time to read this for me, and I'll get the changes made tonight."

"I can read it one more time if you want, but if not, I think you can go ahead and email it to both agents."

"Sounds good."

Traci wished she could tell Simone that she'd called her editor this morning, and that she'd agreed to read Simone's first three chapters. Traci's editor had also told her that if she liked them, she would either read more of the manuscript herself or assign it to another editor who acquired romance titles. But Traci knew it was best to follow her first mind in terms of not saying anything until she had good news. Because if for some reason Traci's editor didn't like it, she wouldn't tell Simone anything.

Traci stood up. "Well, hey, I just heard Tim walk in, so I need to get going. But you have a great evening, okay?"

"I will, and you, too, Traci."

Traci left her office and walked down the long corridor and into the kitchen.

Tim was already removing his navy-blue suit jacket and hanging it across the back of a chair.

He reached his arms out to her. "Hey, baby."

"Hey yourself," she said, hugging and kissing him. "How was your afternoon?"

"Good. After I called you, my boss came in to tell me that we got that five-year distribution contract we placed a bid on last month. So we're all pretty excited about that."

Traci removed a glass dish of baked chicken from the top oven and set it on the granite island. "That's great news."

"It really is, but how was *your* day?"

"It was good."

Traci picked up the pan of broccoli she'd steamed from the stove and poured the content into a serving bowl. Then she pulled two foil-wrapped baked potatoes from the bottom oven and set both dishes next to the chicken.

Tim loosened his tie, opened the first two buttons of his shirt, and sat down.

Traci set out napkins, silverware, and two bottles of Fiji water and took a seat next to him.

Tim held her hand, and they bowed their heads and closed their eyes.

"Dear Heavenly Father," he began, "we come thanking you for the food we are about to receive. I ask that you bless my wife, who has prepared it, and that you allow this food to serve as nourishment for our bodies. In Jesus's name, Amen."

"Amen," Traci said.

Tim reached for the large fork and lifted a couple of thighs onto his plate. "So what are we doing for Easter? Are we having dinner here or going to your parents'?"

Traci spooned out a helping of broccoli. "Mom and I just talked about that this afternoon, and I told her doing it at our house is fine. She's still going to cook most of the food, though."

"Sounds good to me. I love your cooking, but nobody cooks like your mom."

"Don't I know it," she said, and they both laughed.

"Maybe I'll invite Simone and her fiancé over as well. That is, if she isn't going to visit her family in California."

Tim looked at her. "Really? Why?"

"Because she doesn't have anyone here, and you know I hate to see anyone spending the holidays alone."

"What about her fiancé?"

Traci opened the foil around her potato. "Meaning?"

"Doesn't he have family?"

"I don't know. He might, but I still want to invite them. Is that okay?"

Tim sighed. "It's not that I don't want to have them over, because to me the more the merrier. But I also don't want the same thing that happened before to happen again."

"Like what? That crazy drama with Denise?"

"Exactly."

"I hear you, believe me I do. But I really don't think Simone is like that. She doesn't seem like the kind of person who's out to hurt anyone."

"Why is being friends with her so important to you?"

"It's not. But it's like I was telling you yesterday, Simone is a writer. You have your coworkers and other business colleagues who you can converse with almost every day, but I don't have that. I communicate with a few authors online, but ever since that Denise fiasco, I've purposely kept my distance from other writers. I haven't even trusted authors who I can tell are probably good people. All because Denise turned out to be a lot different than I thought she was. I thought she was loyal and genuine, but of course, she wasn't."

"Yeah, and I can understand why. Denise seemed like the real deal to all of us and like she had your back. But all that matters now is that we found out otherwise. She talked about you in ways I never would've imagined, and then when you confronted her she cursed *you* out and hung up the phone. She badmouthed your writing, and she did it at a writers' conference, no less. Almost like she wanted you to hear about it. But worse than that, she lied and told some of her readers that she helped you write your first book. Knowing full well she didn't even know you back then."

Traci heard what Tim was saying, but she still didn't believe Simone had that kind of spirit. She wasn't that kind of person. However, Traci finally responded. "Okay, maybe you're right. If you don't want me to invite her, I won't."

Tim looked at her, this time slightly turning his body toward her. "Look, baby, that's not what I'm saying. I was just curious about *why* you wanted to invite her. But if you really want to, please go ahead."

Traci smiled. "Are you sure? Because it's only dinner, and it's not like I'm planning to have her over all the time."

"It's fine. Really."

"I'm glad, and just so you know, I also asked my editor to read Simone's manuscript."

Tim unscrewed the top of his spring water and took a few sips. "And was she interested?"

"I don't know. She's reading three of the chapters tonight, so we'll see."

"I hope it works out."

"I do, too, because Simone really is a good writer. She has true talent."

Tim cut a piece of his chicken. "That's great to hear, but enough about Simone. How is your own synopsis coming along? I know you were thinking about it this morning before I left."

It was clear that Tim still wasn't all that happy about Traci inviting Simone and Chris over, nor did he understand why she even wanted to be friends with Simone. But it was the same as she'd been thinking before: Simone seemed lonely and unhappy. She didn't sound or act that way, but it was just a feeling Traci had. And when she got those feelings, she was rarely wrong about them. She wouldn't allow anyone to treat her the way Denise had, not ever again, but that didn't mean she couldn't be friends with Simone or that Traci couldn't help her get published. It was true that Denise had caused Traci to lose all confidence in other authors, but it was time to move beyond that—it was time she practiced what she preached by forgiving Denise.

It was time to admit that not all women were self-centered, insecure, jealous, and deceitful, the way Denise was.

Chapter 15

Simone gazed around the beautiful reception area of the pastoral offices. She and Chris had just arrived for their third pre-marital counseling session with Pastor Raymond. But instead of focusing on that, she thought about the way she'd lied to Traci yesterday about working, when she knew she'd never left the house. But it was just that she didn't want Traci thinking she was some lazy slacker who couldn't handle working full-time and putting in as many hours as possible toward her writing career. Still, she hated lying to her, even more so now that Traci had called her back last night to invite her and Chris over for Easter dinner. Simone hadn't been able to believe it, and although nearly twenty-four hours had passed, she was still ecstatic.

Sadly, though, Chris didn't feel the same way she did, and he couldn't stop whining about it.

"I still don't understand it."

Simone looked at him. "Don't understand what?"

"Why you want to go to Traci's house for dinner when my parents invited us over two weeks ago. And you know it's a holiday."

"I know, baby, and I'm sorry. But I really want to go, and I hope you can do this for me just this one time. Traci has been so nice to me. She's gone out of her way to help me get published, and you and I will be spending every holiday with your family from now on. So all I'm asking is that we go over to Traci's for Easter."

Chris looked away from her, straight ahead.

Simone touched his arm. "Baby, are we good? Can you do this one thing for me?"

"Fine, Simone. Whatever you want."

She grabbed his hand, but he didn't react one way or another. Thankfully, it was only minutes before Pastor Raymond opened his door and walked out to greet them.

"So how are the two of you doing this evening?" he asked.

Chris got to his feet and shook Pastor Raymond's hand. "Okay, I guess."

"How are you, Pastor?" Simone asked.

"I'm doing well. Why don't we go into my office and get started."

Simone and Chris followed him inside, and he took a seat behind his desk. The two of them sat in chairs in front of him.

Pastor Raymond relaxed in his chair and clasped his hands together. "So, Chris, I missed seeing you on Sunday."

Simone looked at her fiancé and could tell he felt uncomfortable. Embarrassed, even.

He pulled off his black leather jacket and laid it across the arm of his chair. "Uh, yeah. We visited another church."

Pastor Raymond looked surprised. "Oh."

"But it's not like we're looking for a new church or

anything," Chris hurried to say. "Simone just wanted to visit Pastor Black's church."

"Most people do," Pastor Raymond said. "He's a great man of God and a good friend of mine."

"I know you've talked about that before. You were friends with him well before he turned his life around, right?"

"I was. He's one of the best men of God I know. He's proof that all saints have a past and every sinner has a future."

"I agree," Chris said.

"So, Miss Simone, when are you planning to come to service here at Living Faith? And more importantly, when are you planning to join?"

"I'm not sure," she said, knowing that her heart was now set on becoming a member of Deliverance Outreach—Pastor Curtis Black's church—the church where Traci and her family attended. She knew Chris would be hesitant at first and that it was going to take a lot of convincing for him to leave his current church, but eventually he would. He wouldn't be happy about it, but he would soon realize that Deliverance Outreach was where she belonged. He would see that this was where they *both* belonged as a married couple.

Pastor Raymond and Chris made more small talk, and then Pastor Raymond moved on to the topic of finances. This always made Simone nervous, because to this day, she still had Chris believing she was in management and that she likely earned thousands more than she did. Some men would have wanted to see her pay stubs, what with their preparing to get married, but Chris hadn't seen anything. And Simone was going to keep it that way. Actually, now that she thought about it, with the exception of picking her up for lunch sometimes, he'd never visited her place of employment, something she was glad about because she didn't want him thinking she didn't earn enough money or that she didn't have a prestigious enough job.

"So, tell me, Simone," Pastor Raymond said, "how do you feel about a married couple's finances?"

"I believe a husband and wife should pay their bills together but keep the rest of their money in separate accounts."

"I understand how you feel, but going into a marriage with a yours-is-yours-and-mine-is-mine sort of philosophy is a sure recipe for failure."

Simone stared at him with no emotion. "I disagree."

Pastor Raymond turned to Chris. "And what about you, son? How do you feel about it?"

"I believe all our money should go into one account for bills, and that all the other accounts should be joint as well. I do think it's good for each spouse to have their own retirement account, of course, and maybe one separate checking or savings account, but again, the majority of the money should remain together."

Simone had known for a while that this was the way Chris felt, but whenever he tried to bring it up, she changed the subject. She pretended now too, that she wasn't aware of his feelings about any of this. "I didn't realize you thought this way."

"Well, I do. It's the way my parents have handled their money for forty-five years, and they've never had any money problems."

Simone wanted to tell him that not every married couple was his parents, but she knew he didn't deserve that kind of disrespect. Nonetheless, she still wasn't showing him her paychecks or depositing them into any joint accounts.

Pastor Raymond looked at Simone. "Is this something you're willing to reconsider?"

"No. Not when I know we can still have a great marriage and good money management without pooling everything together."

Chris shook his head in frustration. "I don't believe you."

Simone didn't even bother responding, so Pastor Raymond asked her something else.

"So what about organized religion? Do you feel any different about that than when we first began your counseling sessions?"

"No, not really. But I do want to join a church."

Pastor Raymond smiled. "*A* church or *this* church?"

"I'm not sure."

Chris seemed dumbfounded. "Baby, what are you talking about?"

"Honey, I'm sorry," she said, "but I just don't know if this is where God wants me to be."

Chris raised his eyebrows. "Wow, so let me guess: You now want to join Pastor Black's church. That's what this is all about, isn't it?"

"No," she lied. "I don't know where I want to join, and in all honesty, it could end up being right here. I'm just saying I'm not sure."

Chris sighed and leaned away from her, toward the other side of his chair. She waited for him to say something, but he didn't.

Pastor Raymond flipped through a couple of documents in

their file folder. "Well, it doesn't look like we're making any real progress tonight, does it? But why don't we talk about living arrangements. Have you decided where you're going to live?"

"This seems to be an issue, too, but I don't see why," Chris said. "Not when I have a nice three-bedroom brick home. So it only makes sense that Simone should give up her condo and move in with me."

"Yeah, but I don't know if that's the right thing to do, either. My condo is newer than your home, and it's located in a much better neighborhood."

Chris frowned. "But you're only renting it. I own my house, so why should I have to sell it?"

Now Pastor Raymond sighed louder than normal and leaned back in his chair again. "I don't really know how to say this any other way except to just say it: The two of you have far too many differences to be getting married. You're what we ministers call unequally yoked. And in your case, it's in more ways than one, which is never good."

Simone folded her arms and so did Chris. They just sat there, staring at Pastor Raymond in silence. He didn't seem to know what else to say either, though, so after a few minutes, Chris scooted to the edge of his chair.

"Pastor, I'm really sorry to cut this meeting short, but before we continue our sessions I think Simone and I need to discuss a few things."

"I think that's a very good idea, and I certainly understand. Better to discuss your issues now than to end up in divorce court."

Simone squinted her eyes in anger before she could stop

herself, but Pastor Raymond was getting on her nerves. And as she sat looking at him, she remembered something. She wasn't joining his church anyway, so it wasn't necessary to make a big deal out of this. Not when she knew Deliverance Outreach would become her church home.

Not when she was planning to make that happen sooner rather than later.

Chapter 16

C hris still wasn't all that happy about having Easter dinner with Traci, Tim, and the rest of their family, but Simone was glad he hadn't changed his mind about going. As for her, she'd barely been able to sleep last night because of how excited she was.

Chris turned into the subdivision and made a right at the first stop sign they came to. As they proceeded down the street, Simone looked from house to house, admiring every single one of them. She'd give almost anything to live in this neighborhood. She'd grown up with nothing, and to her, when a person had struggled and gone without so much as a child, he or she deserved to live the best life possible as an adult.

They pulled in front of Traci and Tim's home, and the first thing Simone noticed was how manicured the lawn was. The overall landscaping design was elegant, too, and their three-level brick home with a side-load four-car garage was breathtaking.

Simone raised her sunglasses from her face to the top of her head. "Can you even imagine having a home like this?

I mean, talk about being blessed. And did you see both their vehicles? A Mercedes S550 and a seven-series BMW."

Chris parked close to the curb in front of the house but didn't say anything.

"Baby, are you listening to me?"

"Yeah, but I'm not sure what you want me to say."

"I'm asking if you saw their two cars before you parked."

"No, and I'm not sure how you did, either."

"The garage was wide open. And just look at this house. Just look at it."

Chris turned off the ignition and opened his door.

Simone frowned. "Why aren't you saying anything?"

"Because I don't understand why all this is such a big deal to you. Material things are nice, and I'm happy for Traci and her husband. But I also don't see a reason to lose my mind over it."

"Really? So none of this makes you want a bigger house or a better vehicle?"

"No, because unlike you, I don't spend my time comparing myself to others."

"And what is that supposed to mean? I don't compare myself to anyone, either."

"Whatever you say. Look, let's just go in."

"I don't, and I hope you're not going to walk inside their home with this negative attitude."

"Then stop acting like material possessions are more important than people. Plus, all of this is the least of my worries. What I'm concerned about has to do with us. You and me, and all the differences we still haven't worked out. So maybe I shouldn't go in here at all."

Simone's heart dropped, and she panicked. "Baby, please don't do this. Not today."

"Well, you know it's the truth. We have a lot of problems, and we can't seem to agree on anything. And I'm not in the habit of pretending like everything is great when it isn't."

Simone wasn't about to let him ruin her visit with Traci, so she said, "Okay, you're right. We do have a lot to figure out, so tell me what it is you want me to do."

"You already know."

"What? That you want us to live at your house instead of my condo?"

"Yes, and I want you to join my church, and I want us to have joint bank accounts."

Simone sighed because she knew she would never agree to either of the last two. As it was, she didn't necessarily want to give up her condo, either, but she could at least live with that decision. Still, she saw how serious he was, so she told him what he wanted to hear.

"Fine. I'll do everything you want, and the only reason I've been so guarded and hesitant about everything is because I'm afraid. You know I was engaged once before, and I was very hurt behind it. So it's hard for me to trust you the way I know I can. But no matter what, I want you to know that I love you, Chris, and that I've never loved any man the way I love you."

At first Chris didn't comment, but when he saw tears in her eyes she could tell he believed what she was saying. She hated using drastic measures to get what she wanted, but he hadn't left her any other choice.

Chris caressed the side of her face. "When are you ever going to get beyond these trust issues of yours? I've been honest and caring toward you since the very beginning. I've loved you since day one."

"I know, and I'm working on it. I really am."

"Okay, look. I know this is important to you, so let's just go in and have a good time, and we'll talk about our stuff later."

Simone kissed him, they both got out, and she opened the back door and lifted the German chocolate cake from the seat. Then they walked up the long driveway and down the short sidewalk to the front door. Simone rang the bell and could already see the gorgeous chandelier in the entryway.

Traci opened the door and hugged both of them as they walked in. "Hey, you guys. We're so glad you could make it."

"Thank you so much for inviting us, and here's a little something we brought for dessert," Simone said. "I'm sure you already have more than enough, but I hope you like it."

Traci took the container from her. "I'm sure we will, and dinner is almost ready. Right now, everyone is in the family room."

Simone and Chris followed Traci, and unsurprisingly, the interior of the home was even more beautiful than the outside. It was, by far, Simone's dream home, and if it took her the rest of her life, she would have one just like it.

When they walked into the family room, Traci said, "I know you guys met everyone else when you visited our church, but my nephew, Ethan, was away at school."

Ethan got up and shook Simone's and Chris's hands. "It's nice to meet you both."

"Nice to meet you as well," Chris said.

"Your aunt Traci was telling me that you attend Northwestern," Simone said. "What a great school."

"That it is."

After that, Traci's parents, Earl and Janet; Traci's sister, Robin; and Tim said hello and shook their hands.

But then Robin continued. "When we met you at church, your hair was different, right? You had this really cute cut, and it was very short."

Simone smiled. "Yeah, I'd been wanting to make the change for a while, though."

"So ironic that it looks exactly like Traci's. Same style, length, and even the color."

Simone nodded. "I know, I keep telling her how strange it is that we have so many of the same tastes."

"Well, if that's true, then pretty soon we won't even be able to tell you guys apart," Robin said, laughing.

The room fell silent, but then Traci's mom said, "Simone, it really is great to have you and Chris here. And actually, I just set the last of our dinner on the table."

Everyone began heading out of the family room, but before they left, Simone took note of the beautiful red leather sectional and two matching chairs. She also noticed all the ceramic accessories and contemporary figurines.

Now, as they entered the dining room, everyone took their seats, and Tim said grace. Simone bowed her head and closed her eyes, but she felt a bit out of sorts. She wasn't used to sitting down with a real family, the kind that loved one another and prayed together. She'd had dinner with her future in-laws plenty of times, but there was something different with Traci's family. There was something special about the closeness they seemed to have and how they enjoyed each other's company.

When everyone said "Amen," Traci and Janet began passing dishes, and Simone had never seen so much food. And it smelled so good. Turkey and cornbread dressing, candied yams, mustard greens, potato salad, baked beans, green beans, macaroni and cheese, ham, and fruit salad.

"So," Traci's dad, Earl, said to Chris, "have you lived here in Mitchell all your life?"

"Sort of, but not really. I'm originally from Nashville, but my parents moved here when I was two."

"Nashville is a very nice city."

"It is, and we try to get down there to see my aunts and uncles at least once a year."

Tim scooped out a large helping of dressing and set it on his plate. "We have a plant down there, but I haven't visited it yet. And Traci tells me that you work at the post office."

"I do," Chris said, picking up a couple of dinner rolls with a pair of plastic tongs. "I've been there since graduating high school."

Earl nodded. "That's great. Then you've been there for a while."

"I have."

Robin ate some macaroni and cheese, and then looked at Simone. "Traci tells me that your mother and grandmother live in California."

"Yes, they moved there a few years ago."

"And you'd rather be here for the holiday weekend instead of visiting out in sunny California?"

Simone smiled but didn't say anything, because she was starting to feel as though Robin was purposely picking at her. But finally she said, "Oh my gosh, who made these yams?"

"I did," Janet said.

"Well, they're definitely the best I've ever tasted."

Traci chimed in. "Yeah, we think so, too."

Janet smiled. "Thank you, Simone. I'm glad you like them."

"Actually, everything is good, and I will never be able to thank Traci enough for inviting me and Chris over. And Traci and Tim, your home is absolutely gorgeous."

"Thank you," they both said.

"And...I also hope Chris and I can get a tour before we leave," Simone added.

Chris stopped in the middle of his conversation and glared at her, and she knew he didn't approve of what she'd just said to Traci. But Simone ignored him. Then she looked at Tim and wished Chris would wear button-up shirts the way Tim did. Chris was more of a polo shirt and sweater man, but Simone was going to start buying him shirts with buttons.

Simone also couldn't stop thinking about that red leather sectional that Traci had in her family room, along with her style of accessories. She was still so shocked that she and Traci had such similar tastes. Then, when they'd been on their way to the dining room, she'd gotten a quick peek into the kitchen and had seen their stainless steel refrigerator and microwave. Simone hadn't been able to see the stove or dishwasher, but she was sure they were stainless steel also. Maybe it was best for her to give up her condo after all. If she did, she could replace all of Chris's black appliances with stainless steel ones. She could certainly do the same at her condo, but since she wasn't buying it, it didn't make sense.

Simone chatted with Traci, Janet, and Ethan, and then found herself staring at Traci's wedding ring. It was then that she realized she still needed to find a way to tell Chris that she didn't want the solitaire ring he'd given her. She also had to figure out how to convince him to trade his truck for a Mercedes. And not for a black or silver one, or any other color. Simone wanted white—just like Traci's.

But then, how great would it be, too, if a home went up for sale in Traci's subdivision...on the same street...or better yet, right next door to her? Simone couldn't imagine a more perfect scenario, and maybe if she planned and prayed with her entire being her dream would come to pass. She and Traci would live side by side and become closer than two women who had been friends since childhood. They would share an unmatchable, unheard of, unbreakable bond—the kind that not even blood sisters could speak of.

Six Months Later

Chapter 17

*I*t had taken Simone six months to pull the money together, but she finally had her pure-white S550
Mercedes. Actually, if Chris hadn't been so difficult
and had been willing to trade his truck the way she'd asked
him, she'd have had her brand-new vehicle much sooner.
Well, technically her car was two years older than Traci's, but
it had been a lot more affordable. Yes, it had still cost more
than she'd been comfortable with, and her monthly payment
was far more than she'd been expecting, but she was happy.

Now she was headed to Traci's local book-signing event for
the release of her latest novel. Traci's book had gone on sale
nationwide two weeks ago, and while she'd already traveled
on her ten-city tour, she'd decided to do her Mitchell signing
at the very end.

Simone was excited for Traci, but she couldn't deny feeling
a little envious. She didn't want to feel this way, but a part
of her wished that this were *her* signing, *her* national tour—
her big night. Although, if things continued to go well with
her new publisher, Simone would be selling as many books as
Traci in no time. It had been six months ago, in March, that

she'd submitted her query letter to Michaela and Tanny, and Michaela had offered her representation. Then, not long after that, she had sold Simone's book to a romance publisher. Simone had sort of been bummed about not being offered a contract by Traci's publishing house, though, since that was where she'd wanted to be more than anywhere else. It also hadn't been until after she'd received the offer from her current publisher that Traci had told her how she'd shared Simone's first three chapters with her own editor. But Traci's editor had decided to pass. Traci had insisted, however, that being with one of the most well-known romance publishers in the country was the best place for her, anyway. Simone, of course, disagreed, but it wasn't like she'd had any choice in the matter. This was also the reason her first romance book would also be her last, and she was currently writing a contemporary women's fiction title. That genre was working well for Traci as well as for many other authors, and Simone knew it would work much better for her, too. Plus, she'd recently come to realize that contemporary women's fiction was what she most enjoyed reading. She hadn't thought much about it before meeting Traci, but she wasn't surprised because she and Traci always tended to like the same things.

Simone parked and walked inside the bookstore. She wasn't sure what she'd been expecting, but Traci's signing was standing room only. There must have been two hundred people either sitting or gathering around. Simone had already purchased her book the first day it had gone on sale, which she'd brought with her, so she moved closer to the crowd. She immediately saw Traci's family: Tim, Janet, Earl, and Robin.

"Hey, Simone, how are you?" Janet asked, hugging her.

"I'm fine, Mrs. Calloway. How are you?"

"Great."

"Hi, Mr. Calloway," she said, waving to him. "Hey, Tim. Hey, Robin."

Earl and Tim smiled, said hello, and waved back, but all Robin did was mouth a dry *hello* to Simone. Robin also stared at her and then shook her head, and Simone wondered what her problem was.

So she turned her attention back to Traci's mom. "This is a really great turnout, and on a Tuesday night, even."

"It is, and we couldn't be more proud of Traci. More than that, though, we're grateful to God for blessing her with such kind and supportive readers. That's the reason none of us are sitting. We arrived early, but we want as many of Traci's readers as possible to have seats."

Simone looked toward the front, where Traci was standing, and waved.

Traci smiled and waved as well.

Then one of the bookstore staff members walked over and picked up the microphone from the table.

"Good evening, everyone."

"Good evening," most people responded.

"Tonight, we are honored to welcome nationally bestselling author Traci Calloway Cole."

There was a huge round of applause, but Simone wondered why the staff member was referring to Traci that way. Traci had certainly made a few online bestseller lists, but not even her publisher referred to her as a "nationally bestselling author" on her book jacket. It wasn't that Simone didn't want Traci to be called that, because she did have readers nationwide, but she also didn't like when people exaggerated things or made people sound as though they were more successful than they were.

The staff member continued. "I also think it goes without saying that we are very proud to have one of our own—a Mitchell native—representing our city all across the country. I can still remember Traci's first book release and signing, and it's wonderful to see how much she has grown as a writer and how much her audience has increased. I think at your first signing," she said, turning to Traci, "there were maybe thirty attendees, and then for your second about a hundred, and now look at the amazing crowd who came to support you tonight."

Everyone clapped again, but Simone wondered how much of Traci's success with her local signings had more to do with her being a member of Pastor Black's church than it had to do with her actual stories. Traci was a good writer, but nonetheless, Simone couldn't help being a little skeptical. She was sure that Deliverance Outreach included Traci's new books and events in their general announcements, and this was another reason Simone was going to join there. She'd, of course, wanted to do so before now, but Chris still wasn't interested. If he didn't get on board soon, though, she would join without him. Even if she had to lie and say she hadn't.

"So without further adieu," the staff member said, "I give you Traci Calloway Cole."

The applause was louder than it had been the first two times, and Simone longed for the day when readers would show her the same kind of love and respect.

Traci hugged the woman and took the microphone. "Good

evening, and thank you all so, so much for coming out tonight. I am so completely overwhelmed by your support and generosity, and I am forever grateful. God has certainly blessed me to be able to do what I love, but without all of you...without my readers," she said, becoming emotional, "it never could have happened. Don't get me wrong, I keep my faith in God and I know that I can do all things through Him, but I still know that you have truly helped make an amazing difference in my life. So thank you. Thank you so very much."

There was more applause, and now attendees chattered with others sitting or standing next to them. One woman said, "Amen, Amen, Amen," and Simone wondered if the woman thought she was at church.

Traci looked toward the back of the crowd. "I also want to thank the best parents in the world. Thank you for loving me so unconditionally, supporting me, and raising me up to be the best woman I can be. I will never fully be able to thank you for everything you've done, and I love you eternally. Then, to my sister and only sibling, Robin. What can I say? You are my sister, my confidante, my best friend. You are only five years older than me, but you have been looking out for me and protecting me since we were in grade school together. And I love you dearly. And to the best husband in the whole wide world," she said, taking a deep breath. "Thank you for encouraging me, protecting me, and for loving me in the way every woman should be loved. You are truly my soul mate, and I love you from the bottom of my heart."

Simone looked on as Tim, Robin, Janet, and Earl smiled with the kind of joy she wished she'd had the chance to experience with her mother and grandmother. If only they'd treated her better or had even made some attempt at loving her, she wouldn't have such awful memories of her childhood. If only she'd been given the same love and opportunities as Traci, she'd have a husband, career, and house like hers. She'd have everything she'd ever wanted, and she wouldn't have to drag herself to a job that she could barely tolerate. She also wouldn't have to do what she'd promised herself she'd never do again: dig herself deeper and deeper into debt the way she'd been doing for months.

"Okay," Traci said, now wiping away tears and laughing. "Now that we've got all that out of the way."

Everyone laughed with her.

"So, as you know, *Copycat* is my third novel, and one I really enjoyed writing."

Simone swallowed hard and tried to pretend she wasn't hurt—and disappointed. Had Traci actually passed on acknowledging her? Her own friend? And not just any friend but a best friend?

Traci held up the book. "The story centers on a woman who, after becoming friends with a coworker, begins copying every single thing her friend does. She buys all the same clothing, jewelry, shoes, furniture, and anything else she sees her friend with. She even begins to act like her in a number of different ways and adopts most of her personality traits."

"I know firsthand what that's like," a woman toward the middle of the audience blurted out, and most people laughed. "Oh...and I'm sorry for interrupting you, Traci, but you just don't know how bad things got with this woman I used to be friends with."

"It's fine," Traci said. "My hope is that the story will get a lot of folks talking and sharing their personal experiences."

"Well, I had the same thing happen to me," said another woman.

"Years ago, I had to change departments at work because a woman kept copying everything I did," a lady standing near Simone said. "She even started doing things that I *said* I wanted to do! Even though I hadn't done them myself."

There was more laughter.

"How interesting," Traci said. "I think copycatting is much more common than a lot of us realize, and while I don't think most copycats mean any harm, most people don't like having to deal with it. I also believe that when people become copycats on the level of the character I wrote about, they're dealing with much deeper issues, such as envy and jealousy. They've also lost a great sense of self and their overall identity. They're trying to be something or someone they're not, and a few months ago, our pastor gave a sermon about that. The title was 'Pretending to Be Someone You're Not and the Ultimate Consequences.' And I think this whole subject is very sad. Especially because people who don't know it's okay to be themselves must be very unhappy inside."

Simone listened to the rest of what Traci was saying, and while she'd loved Traci's other two books, she didn't like this one as much. She wasn't sure why exactly, but the story hadn't grabbed her, and she wasn't all that fond of the two main characters, especially the one who copied her friend all the time. The woman was just plain irritating, but Simone still hoped the book did well for Traci.

After Traci finished speaking and reading an excerpt from

her book, she answered questions from the audience. Now she was getting ready to sign books.

"Oh, and one more thing," she said, looking toward the back. "Simone, raise your hand."

Simone had been caught off guard, but she lifted her hand and smiled.

"Everyone, this is my friend Simone Phillips, who is an amazing romance writer. I'm also very excited to announce that Simone has signed a publishing deal, and her first novel will be released next year. So I'm asking that you all please come out to support her signing and that you buy her book."

People applauded for Simone, and while Traci had finally mentioned her to everyone, she was still disappointed. Traci *had* introduced Simone as her friend, but she certainly hadn't raved over her the way she had about Robin or called her a *best* friend.

Simone tried to keep her composure, acting as though this hadn't bothered her, but the more she looked at Robin, the more she wished Traci didn't even have a sister. Simone could also tell that Robin didn't care for her, and that she never had, starting with the day Simone and Chris had joined Traci's family for Easter dinner. She'd given Simone the cold shoulder back then, and she was doing the same thing tonight. Actually, over the last six months, whenever Robin had seen Simone, she'd begun speaking to her less and less, and sometimes Robin pretended she didn't see her at all. But Simone didn't care one way or the other, because the feeling was mutual.

She also still considered Traci to be her best friend, even though Traci hadn't referred to her in that respect—because that's what they were. Best friends, BFFs, and sisters for life—that's what they would be until the end of time.

Chapter 18

After Traci finished signing the leftover stock for readers who weren't able to attend the event, she, her mom, and Robin walked outside. It was almost closing time for the bookstore, so Tim and Earl had gone to get the car. Janet and Earl had ridden there with Traci and Tim, and Robin had driven separately.

But Robin wasn't about to head to her car right away. "T., did you see Simone's eyebrows? How she's gone and gotten them shaped just like yours?"

Traci laughed out loud. "Robin, will you please stop it."

"I'm serious, and that's why when I saw her I shook my head. Mom, didn't you notice it? You couldn't help but to."

"Yeah, I did," Janet admitted. "But I just think Simone really admires Traci as a person, and she always talks about how they have the same tastes."

Robin pursed her lips. "Un-huh, but if that were the case, then why is it that Traci always has everything first? When people have the same tastes, they buy and do the same things without even talking to or seeing each other. But when someone always gets everything *after* they see it, they're nothing more than a copycat."

"I still say it's a form of admiration," Janet reiterated. "And I also don't think Simone sees anything wrong with what she's doing."

"Admiration is a good thing, but that's not what this is. This is some sort of crazed obsession."

Traci leaned against the brick pillar near the entrance of the bookstore with her arms folded. "We all know that Simone copies some of the things I do, but I wouldn't call her crazy or obsessed."

"*Some of the things you do?* How about *everything you do?* As soon as I saw her on Easter, carrying the same Gucci handbag and wearing her hair exactly like yours, I knew she was a copycat. That's why I made that joke about not being able to tell you guys apart. Simone spent all that money getting hair extensions, and that's when the two of you really started looking like the Bobbsey twins."

Traci couldn't help laughing at her sister again, and Janet shook her head.

"Then, a month after that, she started wearing sleeveless dresses—just like you do. And let's not even talk about how she suddenly started wearing the same jewelry as you, the same shoes, and Lord have mercy, she even started wearing your same makeup colors. And you're not even the same complexion."

Traci sighed. "Robin, you really need to stop. Not once has Simone worn the same shade of foundation that I do."

"No, but she now wears the same eye shadow colors, blush, and lipstick, and it doesn't even become her."

Janet pulled her handbag farther into her elbow. "No matter what you say, I still believe Simone is a nice girl who had a very tough childhood. And you can tell she doesn't really have a close relationship with her family, so I feel sorry for her."

Traci agreed. "I do, too. Plus, she really has been a good friend to me the whole six months I've known her."

Janet nodded. "She's been a good friend, and she hasn't done anything to make us think differently."

Robin chuckled, but it was clear that she didn't see anything funny. "Mom, you and T. need to pull your heads out of the clouds. Always trying to give people the benefit of the doubt. Always trying to see the good in people who have issues. And let's not forget that when admiration moves to a certain level, it becomes envy. And ultimately jealousy. And T., you just talked about that very thing at your signing. So I'm telling you both: Simone is eventually going to be trouble. Oh, and I forgot the biggest thing of all. She just bought the same car as yours. It's used, but it's the exact same color and model."

Janet shook her head. "Robin, why don't you leave that poor girl alone?"

"Okayyyy, Mom," she sang. "You and T. can be naïve if you want, but T., that friend of yours is a copycat. She's just like the character in that book you wrote."

"Whatever."

"I'm just telling the truth, because it describes your girl completely. Actually, if you hadn't written that story before you met her, I would've sworn it was her you were writing about."

Traci heard her sister, and while she couldn't deny any of

what Robin was saying, she didn't see how copying a friend on a few occasions made someone a bad person. Even Robin and Traci bought some of the same things every now and then. Traci did admit, though, that when Simone had gotten her hair done exactly like hers and had started buying the same clothes and shoes, it had begun to annoy her, but Traci had soon fixed that problem by rarely shopping with her anymore. She'd also stopped wearing certain items whenever she knew she was going to see Simone. Doing this sort of thing felt kind of petty, but because Traci didn't want the two of them going somewhere dressed alike, the way little girls did, she hadn't seen any other alternative. Traci also knew that Simone hadn't begun posting scriptures every morning until after they'd met, but that didn't bother her because Traci thought it was good for as many people as possible to share inspiring scriptures on social media.

When Tim and his father-in-law pulled up to the front door, Traci and Janet hugged Robin good-bye. Then they got inside the back of the vehicle.

Earl rolled down the front passenger window.

Robin leaned in and hugged her father. "See you later, Daddy."

"See you, sweetie."

Now Robin looked at Tim. "And hey, brother-in-law, you'd better watch out for my sister here, because she doesn't have a clue when it comes to that copycat friend of hers."

Tim and Earl smiled but didn't comment.

"Bye, Robin," Traci told her.

"I love you, too," she said, laughing.

Tim waited for Robin to safely get in her car and pull out

of her parking stall, then he drove out of the lot. It was dark, but he still looked in his rearview mirror at his wife. "Well, I will say this: I tend to agree with Robin. She and I talked about it while you were signing, and you should've seen the way Simone stared at you the entire time. She also seemed like she was sad about something. Then, as soon as you finished your Q-and-A and everyone got up to get in line, she found a seat toward the front. And she just sat there, still staring at you and every reader you chatted with. It was almost like she didn't want to talk to anyone else, because I never saw her speak to anyone except us."

"I noticed the same thing," Earl said. "But maybe she didn't know any of the people who were there."

"I don't know," Tim said. "Maybe not, but with all those women in line, it just seems like she would have struck up a conversation with someone. Or she could've even kept standing next to Mom," he said, referring to his mother-in-law, and then continued to Traci, "And I have to say, baby, I'm still a little shocked that Simone got all that hair added just so it would look exactly like yours. I mean, here I am a man, and even I was stunned by that."

"Well," Janet said to her husband and son-in-law, "I'm going to tell the two of you what I told that other daughter of mine: I feel sorry for Simone. She's engaged, but she acts as though she's all alone in this world. And sometimes when people have grown up in poverty, they see and handle life a lot differently than others."

"I agree, Mom," Traci said, "and that's what I've been saying all along. I'm not saying I like all the copycatting, but outside of that, I really like Simone."

Tim continued down the road, and as he talked more about the book-signing event to his in-laws, Traci uploaded a few photos to her Facebook page. She'd asked one of the bookstore staff members to take them with her smartphone, and they'd turned out well. Traci also wrote a caption, thanking everyone for coming out. Then she browsed through the photos individually and came across the one she'd taken with Simone. But as she studied it, she couldn't help noticing Simone's eyebrows. Because Traci had been so busy at her signing, she hadn't paid much attention to them, but now she saw what Robin had been talking about. The natural shape of Simone's eyebrows was nothing like Traci's, but this new version was identical to them. And with her hair being styled with the same cut and color as Traci's, they actually resembled each other. So much so that looking at Simone felt a bit eerie, and Traci suddenly wondered if maybe Simone did fall into the category of copycats that she'd talked about this evening—the kind who had lost their identities. Traci sure hoped this wasn't the case, but if it was, Simone might need professional help. She would need to speak to someone soon before things got worse.

Chapter 19

Simone drove along the highway with a nervous stomach and shortness of breath. She felt as though she was going to throw up, and she knew it was all because of the way Traci had treated her at the bookstore. Simone never understood why she had to become so attached to certain people, because in the end, she always ended up hurt. When she became friends with someone, she made that person her priority and she was as loyal as anyone could hope for. But over the years, she'd discovered that most people only cared about themselves. It had been that way with her so-called best friend in Ohio, and what if Traci wasn't any different? Simone worried that Ohio was happening all over again. She didn't want to believe that, not when she genuinely loved Traci like a sister, but after watching her in author mode tonight, Simone wasn't sure. Yes, she knew Traci had a job to do, and that she needed to spend time with her readers, but as Simone had sat watching her, she'd heard her tell three different childhood friends that she wanted to go to lunch or dinner with them. Simone had thought it was strange, given the fact that Traci obviously hadn't seen them in a while, but for some reason, she'd seemed thrilled to reconnect with all three women. They'd each exchanged cell numbers with her and taken photos, and it was as if these three *friends* that Simone didn't know had made Traci's day. Traci had also taken photos with every reader who'd asked her to and had acted as though Simone were no more than an acquaintance—she'd treated those childhood friends and her readers as though they were far more important than Simone.

As a matter of fact, it hadn't even been until Simone had finally gotten in line to have her book signed that Traci had taken a photo with her. It had seemed as if Simone were merely some loyal reader and not her best friend. And Simone was hurt by all of it. She was surprised, and she felt a little betrayed.

As she pulled into her driveway, preparing to open her garage, her phone rang. But when she saw the number display on the dashboard, she frowned. It was her grandmother. She didn't like talking to her grandmother on any day, but she especially wasn't in the mood right now. However, the same as always, she knew if she didn't answer, her grandmother would keep calling until she did.

"Hello?"

"Hmmph. This is yet another time I called and didn't have to *keep* callin'. Why you pickin' up the phone so regular these days?"

"I'm fine, Grandma. How are you?"

"Oh, you tryin' to be smart?"

Simone didn't even bother responding.

"Well, the reason I'm callin' is to let you know that ya mama is in the hospital, and you need to come see about her."

Simone blew a loud sigh of disgust.

"What? You got the nerve to be irritated 'cause ya mama is sick? Now I *know* I done heard it all. You really are somethin' else, Miss Thang."

Simone rolled her eyes toward the ceiling of the car. "What's wrong with her?"

"Do I sound like a doctor? That's why I said *you* need to come see about her. Sometimes you ask some of the craziest questions. Like you don't even have a brain in that thick head of yours. But never mind that. When can you get here?"

"I can't."

"Why not?"

"Because I have to work, Grandma."

"And those folks won't let you off to come see about ya mama? Not even if you told them how sick she is?"

"I have some important meetings to attend," Simone said, lying. "If I could miss them I would. But I can't."

"You can do anythang you want. We all can. This is a free country."

Simone wasn't sure what she was supposed to say to that, so she didn't respond.

"After all I did for you growin' up. Yeah, ya mama might be a drug addict, and I know she ain't nevva do squat for you, but she still ya mama. Whether you want to admit that or not, she is. Even one of them Ten Commandments talks about honoring your father and mother. Ya father wat'n nothin' but a lowlife—I mean I nevva got to know him before he died, but if ya drug-addict mama was messin' around with him, I already know he what'n worth a cent. Probably nevva had two nickels to rub together. But when it come to ya mama, you know exactly who she is. She might not 'a been a good mama, but she yours and there ain't nothin' you can do to change that. So I'ma ask you again. When are you gone get here?"

"Grandma, I'm sorry, but I can't."

"Didn't you just hear me talk about those Ten Commandments? About honorin' ya mama?"

Simone wasn't sure why this whole conversation about honoring her mother was more than she could take, but it was. "Well, was LeeAnn honoring me when she used to sneak me out of your house and take me to those drug houses with her? Was she honoring me when she made me give oral sex to those drug dealers for crack? Was she honoring me then, Grandma? I was still in elementary school."

"You always brangin' up crazy stuff from the past. Stuff you shoulda got over a long time ago."

Simone shook her head with tears streaming down her face.

"You still there?"

"I have to go, Grandma, and I'm not comin' to Ohio. Ever again."

"You little uppity, lowdown heffa. I'm sick of you always tryin' to deny us. Pretendin' like you don't have a mama or a grandma. I'll bet you got them people in Illinois thankin' we dead or somethin', don't you?"

Simone saw a car pull up, and she knew it was Chris. She'd totally forgotten that he'd told her he was on his way."

"Grandma, I really have to go."

"Why you in a hurry?"

"I'm not."

"Well, all I know is that if you don't bring yo triflin' behind

to Ohio, you gone be sorry. If you don't come see about ya
mama, you gone have hell to pay. If you force me, I'll make
you regret everythang."

Her grandmother's words made her a bit uneasy, but
Velma had been threatening Simone for two years and had
never made good on it. Mostly because as soon as Simone
sent her a couple of hundred dollars or so, she settled down
and things between them returned to normal—if normal was
what a person could call it.

"How much do you need, Grandma?"

"How much can you spare?"

"Maybe a hundred?"

"That's all you got?"

"Yeah, but I'll have more when I get paid on Friday."

"Then I guess that'll have to do for now. And I still wanna
see you by this weekend."

"But—"

"I don't even wanna hear it," Velma said. "I don't wanna
hear nothin' else about how you ain't comin' here."

Simone wasn't going anywhere, but when she saw Chris
getting out of his truck, she hurried to tell her grandmother
what she wanted to hear. "I'll be there as soon as I can."

"See you then. And don't forget to wire my money.
Tonight."

"Grandma, it's really late."

"I might not be as educated as you, but I know at least a
little about that online stuff. I heard MoneyGram will let you
do it right from ya computer."

"Fine, Grandma. Whatever you want."

"Tonight."

"I will."

"See you this weekend. Bye."

Simone breathed deeply, in and out, trying to settle her nerves and stomach, trying to slow her heart rate, and trying to prevent more tears from rolling down her cheeks. What a night. First she'd been humiliated and dissed by Traci, and now her grandmother had called harassing her. Simone was a mess, but she also didn't want Chris to see her like this or start asking questions, so she had to pull herself together. She had to put on the perfect, happy face that he and everyone else was so used to seeing.

Chapter 20

Simone dropped down on the sofa and turned her body toward Chris. He'd been sitting there, waiting for her to run upstairs to throw on an oversized T-shirt and a pair of leggings.

"So the signing was good?" he asked.

Simone nodded. "It was. But didn't you already ask me that?"

"Yeah, but when we first walked in, you seemed like something was wrong. Like you were upset about something. I don't know. I guess I just expected you to elaborate more."

"No, everything's fine. The question is, is everything good with you? Because you don't usually come by here this late on a weeknight. Plus, the reason you said you didn't want to go to Traci's signing was because you were exhausted."

"I know, but we really need to talk."

"About what?"

Chris scanned the living room. "This."

"Okay, so why are you being so cryptic? What does 'this' mean, exactly?"

"This. All the stuff you keep buying."

Simone scrunched her forehead. "I don't understand. What's wrong with buying things? I work every day."

"I realize that, but your spending is really out of control. And it's getting worse."

Simone wasn't sure where these accusations were coming from, but she didn't like them. "I guess I'm kind of lost. I'm not sure why we're even having this conversation."

"We're having it because we're engaged to be married."

"And?"

"I don't want to start our lives off completely in debt. I also need to know how much you earn every year. You've known for a long time what I make, but you've never offered to give me the same information."

Simone wished he'd stop asking unnecessary questions and just stared at him.

Chris stared back at her. "So?" he said.

"So, what?"

"Are you going to tell me?"

"Why are we doing this right now?" she said, for lack of anything better to say.

"Because we're getting married nine months from now, and it's time we disclose everything. It's time we share the good, the bad, and the ugly."

"At ten o'clock?"

"I'm sorry, but this has really been bothering me. I've always thought it was strange that you've never shared much about your finances. Or about your family, for that matter. But with all this spending, I need to know where we stand."

"Well, don't take this the wrong way, but this isn't about *we*. This is *me*, spending my own money."

"I know it's late and you're probably very tired, so I'm going to pretend I didn't hear what you just said."

Simone folded her arms and looked away from him. And for the first time since she met him, she wished he would leave.

"So you're not going to say anything?"

Simone looked at him again. "First of all, what makes you think I'm overspending?"

Now Chris folded his arms, too. "Why can't you just tell me what I want to know? How much you earn and how much debt you're in."

"And why can't you just answer my question?"

"What? You mean why I think you're overspending?"

"Un-huh."

"Because within the last six months—since you met Traci, I might add—you've purchased this huge red leather sectional that's way too big for your living room, two paintings that belong inside someone's mansion, and a Mercedes-Benz that I know you're struggling to pay for. But what beat everything was when you had the audacity to purchase all those new stainless steel appliances for a condo you don't even own. You're not even planning to buy this place. So why would you do something like that?"

Simone tossed a number of lies through her mind, trying to figure out which of them would work best, but Chris had caught her so off guard, she wasn't prepared. Normally she didn't need to be, since she'd always been good with telling off-the-cuff lies with a straight face, but this was different. The reason? She could tell Chris was serious and that he wasn't going to let up. He was ready to ask question after question if he had to, and she wasn't sure how to handle this. She also didn't know what had gotten into him, and why he was sounding so desperate.

"And why haven't you given me a key? Months keep passing, yet I'm still ringing your doorbell like a stranger. Or I sometimes sit in your driveway, waiting for you to get home."

"Baby, please, let's not do this," she said. "Not tonight."

"No, it's now or never. I've been open and up front with you about everything. Every aspect of my life. And now it's time for you to do the same thing. And you can start by telling me your salary and how much money you owe."

Simone stood up. "This isn't the time for this, and I'd really like you to leave."

"Oh, so it's like that? You claim you're so in love with me, but you're throwing me out? Yeah, okay," he said, getting to his feet.

Simone hated when they argued, something they seemed to do a lot lately. But it was mostly because of all the questions he'd been asking for the last couple of months—questions he wouldn't *stop* asking.

Chris glared at her like he couldn't stand her. "I wonder if Traci really knows just how much of a copycat you are. That you buy things just because *she* has them," he said, eyeing her red leather sectional again. "That's why you never invite her over here, because you know all of this is crazy. I noticed a long time ago that you always visit her instead, or you end up suggesting a restaurant where the two of you can meet for dinner. And I also wonder if she knows that you pay twelve hundred dollars every time you have to get those hair extensions replaced. Just so you can look like her. Or that you spend hours looking at her web site and reading through her social media pages. Or that if you're not doing that, you're browsing department store web sites, searching for clothes and shoes like hers."

Simone struggled to swallow the massive lump in her throat and thought she was going to choke. Not once had she told Chris or anyone else how much she paid her hairstylist. And how did he know what web sites and social media pages she frequented? How did he have a clue about the stores she shopped at? What she did in her own home was nobody else's business—not even his—and this was the real reason she hadn't given him a key.

She wanted to ask him all of the above and then some, but she was afraid of what his answers might be. Except Chris didn't wait for her to ask him any questions at all. He had a lot more to say, and he seemed to be just getting started.

He stood in front of her. "So I'm going to ask you one more time, and one time only. How much do you make, and how much do you owe?"

This night would clearly go down as one of the worst of Simone's life, and she wanted it to be over.

"Chris, look. I've already asked you to leave."

"So that's your answer?"

Simone walked through the short hallway and opened the front door.

Chris followed behind her and slammed it back shut.

"What's wrong with you?" she shouted.

"*You're* what's wrong with me."

"What are you talking about?"

"You and all your lies. All your deceit."

"Chris, I really want you to leave."

"When were you going to tell me that you've maxed out all your major credit cards? And all your store cards, too? When, Simone?"

Simone stretched her eyes wide and wanted to die.

"Yeah, that's right. I saw all your statements, and I also saw that you just opened two of your eight major cards a couple of months ago. But those are maxed out, too. You owe more than *seventy...thousand...dollars* on things you didn't even need. Especially that car you just had to have. And it's funny how you never told me that you needed to put twenty thousand dollars down on it. Yet you still have a payment you really can't afford. At least, I don't see how you could. Not a one-thousand-dollar car note on a forty-nine-thousand-dollar-a-year salary. And that doesn't sound like a manager's salary, either."

"Chris, why are you doing this? And where are you getting all this from?"

"Don't worry about it."

His tone was ice cold, and Simone wanted to break into tears.

"You're a real piece of work," he said. "You know that? Because here you had me thinking you were serious about joining my church when you knew all along you weren't going to. But worse than that, for the last few months you've given me every excuse under the sun why you don't feel like going to church. Claiming Sunday was the only day you had to rest. When this whole time, you've been secretly attending Pastor Black's church every Sunday without fail. That's why there have been times when I've called you right after church, and you take thirty minutes or more to call me back. You always needed time to get home and change so you could pretend like you hadn't gone anywhere. But what hurts me the most, Simone, is the new lease you just signed with your landlord. When I first saw it, I felt like the wind had been knocked out of me, because I knew it meant you were never planning to move out of here. You lied to my face about everything, and I was too naïve to see it. Either that, or I saw what I wanted to see, because I always knew you were keeping secrets. I also knew that you worked hard to be something you're not, and that you don't really have any friends," he said with tears in his eyes. "But I really loved you, girl. I loved you with every ounce of my being, and this is how you did me? This is how you treated me? Like I was nothing special. Like I was the enemy."

"Baby, I'm so, so sorry," she said, looking up at him and grabbing his arm. "I didn't mean to hurt you. I didn't mean to do any of this. I just didn't know if you really loved me."

Chris jerked away from her. "Don't say another word to me, because I'm done. You hear me? I'm done with you for good. Don't call me, don't text me, don't ever contact me again. Oh, and one more thing," he said, pulling something from his pocket. "Here's your key; now give me my ring back."

Simone stared at him in shock.

His face turned even colder than it had been. "Give it to me."

Simone slipped the ring off her finger and passed it to him. She'd half expected he would make some sort of final statement, but all he did was leave.

Simone watched him head down the driveway and get in

his car, and she looked at the key he'd just handed to her. She wasn't sure where he'd gotten it from, but she could kick herself for ever allowing him the chance to figure out the security code to her alarm system. He must have seen her type it in a million times. So not only had he thoroughly rummaged through her desk drawers where she kept all her business documents, including her bank and credit card statements and the weekly church programs from Deliverance Outreach, he'd also searched through the Internet browsing history on her computer. He hadn't missed anything, and she knew he would never trust her again. She knew he was done with her just as he'd said, and that there was nothing she could do about it. She had a mind to beg him to take her back, but she also knew that while Chris was one of the best men she knew and that she loved him, she wasn't *in* love with him. She'd tried with all her might to love him the way he loved her, but she didn't have it in her. She'd never been able to love anyone the way she wanted to, and she knew that wasn't normal. She knew *she* wasn't normal, and this was the reason she kept everything to herself. The reason she kept her business and true feelings as private as possible. The reason she tended to have more sad days than happy ones. The reason she smiled when she wanted to cry. The reason she told many lies—trying to make others believe she was doing much better in life than she was.

So yes, she knew her relationship with Chris was over, and she was willing to accept that, but the more she sat thinking, the shakier she became. What if he hadn't just searched through one or two of her desk drawers? What if he'd rambled through every inch of her desk?

Dear God, she thought, and then rushed upstairs to her bedroom to check her phone. With all that had occurred at Traci's book signing and then with her grandmother, she hadn't checked her email messages. But sure enough, she'd received two emails from her alarm system app: one letting her know that the system had been disarmed at six thirty p.m., a half hour after she'd left for the bookstore, and then another notifying her that it was reset at nine o'clock.

Chris had been inside her condo for two and a half hours... and what if he'd discovered the one thing she'd been trying to hide since leaving Ohio? What if he'd seen that other thing of hers... and told Traci about it?

But he would never do something like that—he would never try to pay her back in such a cruel, harmful way. He just wouldn't. Not Chris—the kindest and most compassionate man she knew.

Chapter 21

*T*raci removed her cup from the Keurig machine and added liquid creamer and two packs of Splenda. She smiled, because if Tim were still home, he would probably ask her if she wanted "some coffee with that cream and sugar." He used cream and Splenda, too, but very little, and he also preferred a couple of shots of espresso because of how strong he liked his morning java—or his afternoon java, for that matter.

She sat down at the island and continued watching the Investigation Discovery channel. It was just after nine, so once she finished drinking her coffee, she was going to get her workout in and then lounge around for the rest of the day. Normally she was up well before Tim left for work, but she was sort of tired from all the traveling she'd done over the past couple of weeks. Last night had been a little exhausting, too, but she wasn't complaining, because nothing compared to how great her readers made her feel. They made her events fun and interesting, and her book signing here in town had been even more special because of how heartwarming it was to see people she'd known most of her life—and to know that after all this time, they still kindly and willingly supported her. There were also many people who attended because they'd met her at church or because they knew Tim, her parents, or her sister, so she was grateful in more ways than one.

Just as Traci was about to turn off the television and head downstairs, someone rang the doorbell. Rarely did anyone drop by so early in the morning unannounced, so she wondered who it was. But as she approached the front entryway, she could already see through the stained-glass window inside the door that a man was standing there with flowers.

"Good morning," she said, smiling.

"And good morning to you," the older gentleman replied. "Are you Traci Calloway Cole?"

"I am."

"Then these are for you."

Traci took the beautiful yellow roses from him. "Thank you."

"You're quite welcome. Have a good day."

"You too."

As she closed the door, she wondered who these lovely flowers could be from. She knew they couldn't be from Tim, because, one, he'd already sent her a dozen roses yesterday to celebrate the end of a great book tour, and two, he never sent her any other color except red.

Traci set the tall glass vase on the counter and opened the envelope. She pulled out the card and smiled.

To my best friend, Traci.
Congratulations on the success of your book signing

last night, and please know that I am so very proud of you and all your accomplishments.

Love,

Simone

"How kind," Traci said out loud, and then she walked over to the island and picked up her cell phone. She dialed Simone's number, and Simone answered right away.

"Thank you so, so much for sending the gorgeous roses," Traci said. "They're absolutely beautiful."

"You're quite welcome.

"It was very thoughtful, and I appreciate you thinking of me."

"You deserve them, and I really enjoyed being at your signing last night. So many people came out."

"They did, and I can never thank them enough. It'll be the same way for you, too, though. Your book is great, and it's going to do very well. I even think it'll make the *New York Times* list, because it's such a touching love story. Plus, I'll definitely be promoting it on all my social media pages, in my newsletter, and at all my events. I still have quite a few more scheduled between now and your release date."

"Gosh, Traci. All I can say is thank you, but let's be clear about something. I don't see how I could ever make that list if you haven't."

"Why? Because I have three books out? That doesn't mean anything. Some authors make the list with their first novel, and I really think you're going to be one of them."

"I don't see it, but thank you for being so positive."

"It's the only way to be, and I'm not joking when I say you have an amazing book."

"Well, I'm glad you feel that way, and actually, I need some good news right now. More than ever."

Traci took a seat back at the island. "Why, what's wrong?"

"Chris broke off our engagement."

Traci scrunched her eyebrows. "You're kidding! Why?"

"It's a long story, but I'm having a really hard time dealing with it."

"I am so, so sorry. Chris seemed like such a wonderful guy."

"Yeah, I thought he was, too, until he broke up with me last night for no reason."

"What did he say?"

"That he couldn't be with a woman who couldn't commit to having all joint bank accounts with her husband. And he was also upset because I wanted to join Deliverance Outreach. Chris wanted me to join his church, and he said he couldn't marry a woman who wanted to attend somewhere else."

"He ended things with you because of that? Because you wanted separate accounts and wanted to attend a different church? How strange is that? I mean, Tim and I have joint everything, but it just seems like you guys could've found some sort of compromise about that."

"I know, but he wasn't interested. He wanted things to be his way or no way."

"Gosh. I had no idea you were even having those kinds of disagreements."

"They've been going on for a while, but I never thought he would break up with me over them. But it's okay."

"I know you're saying that, but I can tell you're devastated. I can hear it in your voice."

"It's tough, but I'll be fine. I have to be."

"When did this happen?"

"Right after your signing. He came by when I got home. Actually, when he'd told me he was too exhausted to come to the bookstore, I'd thought something was wrong. But never in my wildest imagination was I thinking he was going to call things off between us."

"Wow, I just can't get over this, because Chris really seemed like a wonderful guy. I know I keep saying that, but he did. Which just goes to show that you never know how people are. You never know who you can trust anymore, and I hate that."

"You're right, and so do I."

"Are you getting off at your usual time?" Traci asked.

"I am, if not before."

"Then why don't I pick up some food and bring it over. That way you won't have to spend the evening alone."

"Well, if you wanna know the truth, I'd much rather come visit you or go to a restaurant. Because being at home is only going to remind me of Chris and what I thought we had. We didn't live together, but he was over all the time."

"I understand. Well, coming here is fine, and I'll just have something delivered. Plus, Tim won't be home until around six thirty tonight, so we were planning to order carryout, anyway."

"Thank you so much for doing this, Traci. Thank you for being my friend."

"Of course. I'm here for you, girl, for as long as you need me to be."

"See you soon."

"You hang in there."

"I will."

Traci set her phone down, trying to wrap her mind around what Simone had just told her. Traci truly felt sorry for her, because what a blow this must've been. One minute thinking someone was in love with you, and the next, learning that he no longer wanted to get married. But again, Traci still couldn't get over the way Chris had obviously changed, because none of what Simone had told her sounded like him—which made Traci wonder if there was more to the story. She didn't think Simone was lying, per se, but maybe something more serious had happened between them and Simone didn't feel comfortable sharing it with Traci. Either way, she was going to be there for her friend just as she'd told her. She would help Simone through this any way she could.

Chapter 22

Simone had just walked inside her condo. She'd thought about going straight over to Traci's right after work, but then she'd decided she wanted to change into something more comfortable. Before Traci had called her, she'd felt a little down about her breakup with Chris, but when she'd learned how much Traci cared and wanted to support her, her spirits were lifted. Just last night, she'd been questioning Traci's loyalty to her as a friend, but now she knew her thinking had been irrational. Traci had simply been busy with her readers and hadn't purposely tried to snub Simone in any way. She would never do that because it wasn't who she was, and Simone would never suspect something like that about her again.

Simone grabbed her purse, but as soon as she did, her doorbell rang. She certainly wasn't expecting anyone, and when she opened the door her stomach turned flips. It was Chris, and she could barely look him in the face.

"Can I come in?" he asked.

Surprisingly, his tone and demeanor were noticeably polite, so she wondered if maybe he'd had a change of heart and wanted to work things out.

But when he closed the door behind him, his calm look turned furious. "So is it true?"

"Is what true?"

"That you got busted in Ohio for selling prescription drugs? Illegally, that is. And that you were locked up in jail until you finally agreed to snitch on your partners? And the state gave you total immunity? Is it true?"

Simone's chest heaved up and down faster than normal, and she wanted to deny all that he'd asked her about. But she could tell he already knew too much. "Who told you that?"

"Your grandmother."

"What?"

"Yeah, your grandmother. The woman who lives right over in Ohio? The woman who doesn't live all the way in California the way you claimed."

Simone stared at him, trying to find the best words to say, but she couldn't.

He half squinted his eyes. "You are by far the biggest liar I know. You know that? And you make me sick. Oh, and your grandmother also told me that she called you last night to tell you about your mom being in the hospital, but you said you were too busy to come see her."

"That's not what I told her, and you don't know the kind of history I have with my mother. You've only heard my grand-mother's side of it."

"Then why did you lie about where they live?"

"Because they've never treated me like family."

"Well, given the way you've treated me and knowing what a huge liar you are, I don't blame them."

157

"You really don't know my mother and grandmother. You know nothing at all, so please don't judge me."

"I know you lied to me about where they lived. You lied about why you left Ohio, you covered up all the criminal activity you were involved in, and look at all the lies I just caught you in last night. And now I know why you spend beyond your means. Why you have to have everything Traci has."

Simone had tolerated about as much as she could take from Chris, and if he kept badgering her the way he was, she would have to throw him out. "Why?"

"Your grandmother told me that trying to keep up with another friend you had in Ohio is the reason you started selling drugs. She said you had a sports car, a luxury car, and a five-bedroom house just like your *friend*, but that when they arrested you they took everything. She also told me that you copied everything she did and that you became so clingy and obsessed with her, she had to cut you off. But even then, you stalked her, and she had you arrested. So imagine how stunned I was to learn all this about you."

Simone couldn't take any more. "Chris, I want you to leave. I'm sorry that things didn't work out between us, but I need you to go. If you don't, I'm calling the police."

Chris opened the front door. "You know, at first I felt bad about stealing your key, but now my only regret is that I didn't do it sooner. I've known for months that you kept a spare in your kitchen drawer, but it wasn't until two nights ago when you were in the shower that I decided to take it. And boy, did I get the surprise of a lifetime. I found your grandmother's number, and today, she sang like an opera legend."

"I'm giving you ten seconds to get out. I mean it, Chris."

He shook his head, laughing. Then he became so serious, she got scared. "You're an awful person, Simone. The worst. But I'm going to make sure you get everything you have coming to you. Everything and then some."

Chapter 23

Traci saw that Tim was calling and picked up the phone. "Hey, baby."

"Hey, I'm on my way, so what's for dinner?"

"I ordered lasagna, fettuccine, spaghetti, and salad from Big Italy's, and they just delivered it."

"Sounds good to me, but that sure is a lot of food."

"Simone is coming over."

"Oh. Is everything okay?"

Traci opened all the bags and pulled out each of the four foil pans. "No, not at all. Chris broke up with her."

"Really? Why is that?"

"Something about her not wanting to have joint bank accounts when they get married. She also doesn't want to join his church, and I guess he wasn't happy about that, either."

"Hmmph," Tim said. "Let me guess. She wants to join our church instead."

"Yep."

"Well, I haven't been around Chris a lot, but that doesn't sound like him to me. He seems much more reasonable than that."

"I thought the same thing, but according to Simone, he basically called things off for no reason."

"Very strange, and somehow I bet if we ask Chris, the story might be a little different."

"That could be, and I do think something else happened. So maybe Simone will eventually tell me."

"Hey, you won't believe this," Tim said. "Chris is calling me."

"Really?"

"Hold on a minute."

Traci pulled three plates and three glasses from the cupboard and set them next to the food containers. She knew Tim and Chris had exchanged numbers a few months ago, but as far as she knew, they never talked on the phone. So she couldn't imagine that Chris was calling to tell Tim about his and Simone's breakup. Traci and Simone were friends, but Tim and Chris only got together because of the two of them.

After a minute or so, Tim came back on the line. "He's on his way over."

"Here?"

"Yep."

"For what?"

"I don't know exactly, but he said it was important."

"Did you tell him that Simone was on her way here, too, and that this probably isn't a good time?"

"I did, but he said that he has something to show us. And that it's all about her, anyway."

"What does that mean?"

"I don't know."

"That sounds really bizarre. What else did he say?"

"That he was sorry he didn't call us last night, right when he figured out what Simone was up to."

"Okay, now I'm really lost. And I sure hope Chris isn't planning to start trouble with Simone when he gets here."

"I don't think that's why he's coming. That's not how it sounded."

"Maybe I should call and warn Simone."

"Look, baby, I know that's your friend, but let's just see what Chris has to say first."

"I don't like this."

"Well, I'm pulling into the driveway now, and Simone just parked in front of the house."

"Okay, I'm hanging up."

Traci heard Tim letting up the garage, so she opened the door between the garage and the kitchen. Once he drove forward and turned the ignition off, he got out and spoke to Simone, who was walking toward him. Then the two of them walked inside the house.

Simone hugged Traci in tears.

Traci hugged her back. "What's wrong?"

"Everything," Simone said, sobbing.

Tim and Traci looked at each other, neither of them knowing what to say.

But then they heard the doorbell ringing, and Tim went to answer it.

"Simone, I hate to tell you this, but that's Chris at the front door."

"Excuse me? For what?"

"We don't know. He called Tim and said he had something to show us, and that it was about you."

Simone opened her mouth to speak, but Tim and Chris walked into the kitchen.

"Chris, why are you doing this?" Simone asked. "All that stuff my grandmother told you was none of your business. It's not anybody's business unless I tell people myself."

"That's not why I'm here," he said, refusing to look at her. Instead, he pulled a set of documents from one of two large envelopes he was carrying and passed them to Traci.

"What are these?" she asked.

"Photos of every room in your house and photos of every room in Simone's condo."

Traci looked at each and every photo. If she hadn't seen them with her own eyes, she never would've believed it. Simone's living room was identical to Tim and Traci's. Her master bedroom was identical to Tim and Traci's. Her guest bedroom looked just like Tim and Traci's, and even Simone's office had the same furniture that Traci's had. In some cases, Simone had been forced to improvise, but even when she had, she'd found pieces that were so similar one could hardly tell the difference. She'd even found similar accessories for every room, and every single color scheme in the various rooms matched Tim and Traci's. The only variation was that the rooms in Simone's condo were a lot smaller than the ones in Tim and Traci's house, although that hadn't seemed to matter to Simone at all. She'd still packed in everything she could. She'd cloned the inside of Tim and Traci's home in a way that didn't seem possible, but more important, what she'd done was insane.

Traci finally looked at Simone. "So every time I invited you here, you were taking photos and using them to redecorate your condo?"

"Traci, you know we have the same tastes. With everything."

"No, we really don't. Not at all, and actually, I've never bought a single thing you have. Plus, Tim and I had all our furniture and accessories well before I met you. Not to mention, when I came to your condo back in March, it looked completely different than it does today."

"Chris, I can't believe you did this!" Simone said, beating him on his chest. "Why are you trying to destroy me? Why are you trying to ruin my friendship with Traci?"

Chris pushed her arms away from him. "Don't touch me," he said, and passed a much thicker stack of documents to Traci. "This is what I'm most sorry about. And I just couldn't let Simone do this to you. I couldn't let her get away with it."

"I'm almost afraid to look," Traci said, "because if it's any worse than what I've already seen, I'm not sure I can take it."

"I took photos of the first three chapters of Simone's next book. And here's a copy of one of *your* books with all the character names highlighted."

Traci scanned a few pages. "Oh...my...goodness. Simone, is this some kind of joke? You're actually copying the story line of my first novel? And basically just changing the names of the characters and using a pen name? Are you crazy? You've got the nerve to be smiling in my face and trying to steal my work? Are you kidding me?"

Tim took the first couple of pages from Traci and skimmed through them. Then he glared at Simone, who was in tears. Now he looked back at Traci. "Didn't I tell you to be careful with this woman? I told you that from the very beginning."

Simone clasped her hands together in front of her chest. "Traci, please let me talk to you. I'm begging you. Please let me explain why I did this. I promise you, it's not what you think."

Traci set the photo version of the manuscript on the island. "Simone, all I want is for you to get out of our house and to never come back."

"Traci, you don't mean that. You're just upset."

"I do mean it. Now get out before I have you arrested."

"Well, it's not like she's never been to jail before," Chris said. "That's for sure."

Simone stormed by him, heading back toward the garage. "Just shut up, Chris. Or even better, why don't you do all of us a favor and just die?"

Tim went and opened the door. "Okay, that's enough, Simone. It's time for you to go. Now."

Simone didn't say another word. All she did was stare at Traci, begging her with tearful, pleading eyes. But when Traci stared back at her with no sympathy, she cried like a child. She fell completely apart and finally left.

She drove away, and Traci vowed to never speak to her again. Not for as long as she lived.

Epilogue
Six Months Later

I t was one year ago today that Traci and Simone had met at Marie's Hair Salon. It had been a normal Thursday evening in March, but little had Traci known she'd been headed toward massive drama. She'd heard about women who mimicked their female friends, but never had she believed she would meet someone on the level of Simone. Simone had taken *everything* to major extremes, and Traci had to admit, she hadn't fully seen it coming. Yes, she'd known within the first couple of months of their friendship that Simone tended to order the same food as her every time they went to lunch or dinner, but Traci hadn't seen anything strange about it. Of course, in hindsight, she now knew that it hadn't been as normal as she'd thought. Maybe if a person occasionally ordered the same thing as one of her friends, that would be one thing, but to do so every single time at every single restaurant, well, that was a bit different. Then, when Simone had changed her entire look, including the way she dressed and wore her hair, Traci had noticed that, too, but she still hadn't thought it was going to be a problem. Traci certainly hadn't liked the idea of someone monitoring every detail of her physical being, along with all other aspects of her life, but she'd tried her best to look beyond those particular oddities. Because after all, Traci and every other person on the planet had their quirks, habits, and differences.

No two people were the same, and Traci had chosen to focus on all the good qualities she'd seen in Simone. Robin hadn't liked Simone from the beginning, and Tim had voiced his concerns very early on, too, but Traci had thought they were both blowing the whole Simone matter out of proportion, and so had Traci's mom. Although, Traci couldn't deny that it was her mom who she'd adopted this whole try-to-see-good-in-everyone philosophy from. Traci didn't necessarily think that was a bad thing, but now that she'd misjudged not one but two so-called friends, she knew it was time to start seeing people for who they were—right when she met them. For most of her life, she'd been a noticeably good judge of character, but for reasons she didn't understand, she clearly hadn't been when it came to Denise and Simone. Maybe it had to do with the fact that after she'd left corporate America, she'd missed having friends who were coworkers—something she had discussed with Tim many times. But even so, this never should have caused her to want to befriend an author so badly that she was willing to overlook obvious and sometimes consistent personality issues.

Of course, nothing compared to all the photos Chris had taken and shown Traci and Tim. No matter how much time had passed, Traci still couldn't believe that Simone had spent so much money and energy on replicating their home. It just didn't make sense to even want to do something like that. But the drop-the-mic moment had occurred when Traci had read those manuscript pages and realized her "friend" was plagiarizing her work and planning to sell it. Her "friend" who she'd helped as much as she could had gone behind her back as though it was nothing.

But what Traci found comfort in now were the words her mother had been telling her since she was a child: "For everything bad, something good always comes out of it." To this day, Traci had never seen that belief proven wrong. Yes, her experience with Simone had turned out to be a nightmare, and Traci had spent the last six months despising her and wishing she'd never met her, but as of last month, she'd gotten past it. She'd prayed hard to forgive Simone, and she finally had. For a while, she hadn't been sure she could, but it was her mom who'd kept reminding her that she hadn't raised Traci to be resentful and unforgiving. She'd taught Traci to love people in spite of their faults, just as God loved her.

Her mother had also insisted she not forget the kind of life Simone had lived as a child. Her mom wasn't dismissing the bad choices Simone had made, but she insisted that when a person hadn't received a certain amount of love and affection as a child, it could set the course for a not-so-great adulthood. Then, when Traci had told her mother about the voice message Simone had left her two weeks ago, apologizing and sharing the truth about what her mother and grandmother had subjected her to—and also saying she knew she had a problem, was seeing a psychologist, and had moved to Atlanta—her mom had felt even more empathy for Simone. Traci had felt the same way, and although she had no proof that Simone was, in fact, in counseling and getting the help she needed, Traci had thought about her a lot and had tried to imagine how hard things must have been for her as a small girl.

Traci knew she and Simone would never be close friends again because too much had happened, but she had genuinely forgiven Simone and was hoping for the very best for her. Later today, Traci would even take the time to tell her by phone, but the important thing was that Traci's decision to forgive Simone had given her a noticeable sense of peace. She felt free and relieved, and she knew it was because she'd done what God wanted all of His people to do: forgive and truly mean it. Let bygones be bygones and move on—regardless of how unkindly someone had betrayed or deceived you. This was exactly what Traci was doing, and she was a better person because of it, which meant everything truly did happen for a reason, and for that, she was grateful.

Six months had passed, yet Simone still couldn't believe how horribly things had turned out for her—and sadly, how cruel of a man Chris had become. He'd seemed so kind, loyal, and loving, but in the end, he'd betrayed her much more callously than her last fiancé had. He'd proven that even the most unsuspecting people might ease a knife in your back when you weren't looking. He'd known how important Traci was to Simone and that their friendship had meant everything to her, yet he'd done all he could to sabotage it. Worse, he'd secretly interrogated her heartless grandmother and then set out to destroy Simone in more ways than she'd counted on.

He'd told Traci and Tim everything, and Simone would never forget the disappointed and disgusted look on Traci's face. Her outrage had been so disturbing that Simone had hardly been able to stand it. And for that reason, she'd left almost as soon as Traci had told her to get out. Simone had certainly wanted to stay and explain things, but the pain and anger in Traci's eyes had told her it wouldn't make a difference.

If only she hadn't tried to use Traci's book as an outline for her next novel, especially since her own book was already receiving stellar reviews and would be published early next year, maybe their friendship could have been salvaged. Because there was no way Traci would have stopped speaking to her simply because she had the same taste in furniture and accessories. She also couldn't see Traci judging her because of the financial trouble she'd gotten herself into while living in Ohio. Not when Simone had been treated so badly by her mother and grandmother since the day she was born. But she'd still found the strength to rise above all that she'd endured—starting at the age of eleven.

It had taken a lot of years and willpower; however, after meeting a schoolmate in sixth grade by the name of Bethany, Simone had decided right away that she was going to be better than her family. She would work hard to get good grades, and she would have everything Bethany and her parents had.

She could still remember the first time Bethany had invited her over for dinner and how she'd never gone inside a house more beautiful. She'd never met a husband and wife who treated their children as though they were the most important people in their lives. She'd never seen a bedroom closet like Bethany's, filled with three different sets of apparel: play clothes, school clothes, and church clothes. Bethany also had shoes for every occasion. And her white canopy bed, which was covered with a gorgeous pink comforter, shams, and pillows, had made Simone want to move in with her—for good. She'd wanted to forget about her own pathetic life and live the same as Bethany and her parents. Simone had wanted this more than anything because she'd known, right then and there, that having money, residing in a nice home, and wearing expensive clothing was the real reason Bethany was so well liked by the children at school. Even their teacher, Mrs. Johnson, had regularly complimented the dresses Bethany wore.

So from that year on, Simone had made up her mind to become somebody. To watch and learn from the people who everyone loved and respected so noticeably. And over the years, she'd done okay. Sure, she'd experienced a few snags along the way, but she always overcame them. She'd lost her best friend in Ohio and done the same with Traci, but the good news was that she was making a new start. Just one month ago, she'd transferred her job again, this time to Atlanta, and strangely enough, she was also seeing a psychologist. She didn't necessarily feel as though she was struggling with any unusual mental or emotional issues, but she did believe that maybe her mother and grandmother had done more damage to her than she'd realized. She'd decided that maybe working through some of her resentment and finding a way to forgive them might make a difference. Because, after all, she was still hoping that Traci would eventually forgive *her*. She knew there was a chance that this might not happen, but she remained optimistic. She was still counting on the fact that Traci had been a true friend to her, and that they had so much in common. They'd found a connection like no other friends she knew of, and Simone missed that.

171

Although, losing two best friends, one after the other, did make her wonder what she might be doing wrong—why she couldn't seem to get things right in that respect. So maybe her counselor could help her with that problem as well.

Simone could only hope and pray for that, and maybe it was finally time, too, that she went to church more often and for the right reasons. Time she genuinely trusted and depended on God. Traci and her family certainly did, and they were happy. In all honesty, the same had been true of her grandmother's next-door neighbor, the woman who had taken Simone to church when she was a child. Miss Mattie had always been a smiling, pleasant, and very caring woman who loved everyone, and Simone would never forget her.

So yes, she was going to find a church home in Atlanta, read her Bible more, and get the emotional help she needed. She would do all she could to become a better person—a fulfilled human being, and most of all, a truly happy one.

Acknowledgments

Twenty-two years ago when I wrote my first book, it never dawned on me that I would write 25 of them. So needless to say, this has been one of the greatest blessings God has given me. From the time I was a small child, my mom, Arletha Tennin Stapleton, and maternal grandparents, Clifton, Sr. and Mary Tennin (the absolute best mom and grandparents who I couldn't have loved more and still miss tremendously) taught me to love, trust, and honor God, and I am forever grateful to them for that. I am, without a doubt, eternally thankful to God for all that You have been to me, what You continue to be, and for what I know You will be to me always.

To the man who I love with all my heart and soul, Will M. Roby, Jr. (my Roby). We have now celebrated 26 wonderful years of marriage, and nothing feels better than being able to say the following heartfelt words to you: I don't just love you, but I am still totally and completely *in* love with you. You still make me smile and laugh every single day of my life, and I will never be able to thank you enough for encouraging me, back in 1996, to start my own business so I could self-publish my first novel. Being rejected by literary agents and publishing houses had certainly discouraged me to the point of wanting to give up, but with Mom insisting that I had to keep trying, and with your supporting me 150% and borrowing money from your 401K account so that I could move forward, well, that changed everything. Your love, faith, and belief in what you thought could happen made all the difference, and what an amazing journey this has been for both of us. You have traveled on every single tour for every single book, and that has given me the kind of peace and joy that I will never fully be able to explain. Thank you, my dear Roby (my love, my best friend, my confidant), for everything. You are my wonderful gift from God.

To my brothers, Willie, Jr. and Michael Stapleton (and my dear sister-in-law, Marilyn), mere words cannot express the love and appreciation I have for you, but thank you for the love, encouragement, and support you have given me since you were small boys. Yes, I am eight and six years older than you, respectively, but to hear you say from the beginning how proud you were of your big sister has always meant the world to me. Then, once we lost our sweet, beautiful mom, I saw how the two of you began to love and respect me more like a mother than a sister, which is why even as I type these words my eyes are filled with tears. I love you both with all my heart, and I thank God for you.

To my stepson, daughter-in-law, and grandsons: Trenod Vines-Roby, LaTasha Vines, Alex Lamont Knight, and Trenod Vines, Jr. To my brothers-in-law and sisters-in-law: Gloria Roby, Ronald Roby, Terry and Karen Roby, Robert and Tammy Roby, and James Roby (who is gone but certainly not forgotten). To all my nieces and nephews: Michael Jamaal Young, Malik Stapleton, Ja'Mia Young, Ja'Mel Young, Shelia

Farris, William Stapleton, Nakya Stapleton, Kiera Holliman, Nyketa Roby, Lamontrose Love, Krissalyn Love, Bianca Roby, Shamica Newkirk, Brittany Roby, Demario Sorrells, Talia Brown, Amaya Love, Kristen Love, Malachi Love, Kasondra McConnell, Kaprisha Ballard, Kiara Bullard, and Ronald Roby, Jr. (who is also gone but not forgotten). To my aunts and uncles: Fannie Haley, Ada Tennin, Ben Tennin, Mary Lou Beasley, Charlie Beasley, Vernell Tennin, Ollie Tennin, Marie Tennin, Shirley Jean Gary, Ed Gary, Ruby Gary, Lehman Gary, Thressia Gary, Rosie Norman and Isaac Gary. To all my cousins and other family members (far too many to list by first names): Tennins, Ballards, Lawsons, Stapletons, Youngs, Beasleys, Haleys, Greens, Robys, Garys, Shannons, and Normans—I will never be able to thank any of you enough for supporting me year after year after year. Your love and encouragement have sustained me as your family member and as a writer, and I thank God for ALL of you. There is nothing like family, and I love each of you with all my heart.

To my first cousin and fellow author who is certainly more my sister than anything else: Patricia Haley-Glass. We have shared an amazing bond and strong sisterhood since we were toddlers, and I love you dearly. You have prayed for me and encouraged me for many years, and I thank God for you. Thank you for everything, Pat. I love you, too, Jeffrey and Taj.

To Kelli Tunson Bullard (and Brian) my best friend and sister for 45 years. Our daily conversations (sometimes multiple times per day) continue to mean the world to me, and I am beyond blessed to have you in my life. Thank you for everything, Kel. To Lori Whitaker Thurman (and Ulysses), my best friend and sister for 30 years. We have had some truly great times, and

Acknowledgments

I am beyond blessed to have you in my life as well. Thank you for everything, Lori. And to my cousin, Janell Green, for being my family and also for being such a dear friend. After twenty-five books, you still read every single manuscript and then call me for no less than a two-hour call with such detailed and helpful feedback. So to Kelli, Lori and Janell—I love all three of you ladies so very much, and I thank God for you.

To a few more women who have been my special sisters for years: Venita Sockwell Owens, Gwyn Gulley, Danetta Taylor, April Farris (my soon-to-be sister-in-law!), Karen Young, Mary Mack Scott, Aileen Blacknell, Veronda Johnson, Regina Taylor, Cathrine Watkins, Valerie Hanserd, Cookie Givens, Mattie Holden, Emily Sanders, Lesia Smith, Janet Salter, Pamela Hanserd, Venae Fowler Jackson, Pamela Charles, Trisha R. Thomas, Trice Hickman, Marissa Monteilh, Tanishia Pearson-Jones, Veronica Hanson Blake, and Tanya Marks Hand— thank you for your friendship, sisterhood and support. I love you all.

To the first readers of the initial manuscript for this book and for most of my other titles: Lori Whitaker Thurman, Janell Green, Connie Dettman, Dr. Betty Price, and LaTasha Vines—thank you for taking time from your busy schedules to read my work and give such helpful feedback. I so very much appreciate all of you.

To Pastor K. Edward Copeland, Mrs. Starla Copeland, and our entire New Zion Missionary Baptist Church family— thank you for all the love and support you continue to give Will and me as members. I love you all so very much.

To my wonderful spiritual mom and family: Dr. Betty Price, Apostle Frederick K.C. Price, Angela Evans, Cheryl

Acknowledgments

Price, Stephanie Buchanan, Pastor Fred Price, Jr., Angel Price, and the entire Crenshaw Christian Center family— thank you for everything, and I love you all so very much.

To my amazing attorney, Ken Norwick, my wonderful publisher, Hachette/Grand Central Publishing—Beth de Guzman, Linda Duggins, Jamie Raab, Elizabeth Connor, Caroline Acebo, Maddie Caldwell, Stephanie Sirabian, Kallie Shimek, the entire sales and marketing teams, along with everyone else at GCP—thank you all for everything and then some. I am truly honored that you are publishing my 25th book and blessed to be one of your authors. To my talented freelance team: Connie Dettman (I love and miss you already, but I am so happy and proud of your new career endeavors), Luke LeFevre, Pamela Walker-Williams, and Ella Curry—thank you for doing all you can to help keep things running so smoothly with my writing career. Each of you are a God-send for sure.

To *all* the bookstores and retailers, *every* radio host, radio station, TV host/anchor, TV station, newspaper, magazine, blog, book reviewer, web site, and other online entities that sell and/or promote my work—with special thanks to the wonderfully kind Emma Rodgers, former owner of Black Images Book Bazaar in Dallas, TX, Frances Utsey, former owner of Cultural Connection in Milwaukee, WI, and all the other independent bookstore owners who sold my books even when I first self-published; to independent owners Kim Knight of Between the Lines Bookstore in Baton Rouge, LA, and Donna and Donya Craddock of The Dock Bookshop in Fort Worth, TX, for continuing to host such fabulous book-signing events for me today; to Andy Gannon and Aaron Wilson at WIFR-TV and Stone & Double T at WXRX (104.9)

Acknowledgments

in Rockford, IL, for interviewing me for every single book release, and the *Rockford Register Star* for all your support since the beginning; to Patrik Henry Bass and *Essence* magazine for two decades of such unwavering, awesome support; to Jeremy Mikula and the *Chicago Tribune* for the amazing and very kind article you wrote and published in July 2016; to Maggie Linton of *The Maggie Linton Show* on XM Radio, Julee Jonez at KPRS-FM in Kansas City, MO, Twanda Black at WALR (Kiss-104.1) in Atlanta, GA, Kimberly Kaye at WFKS-FM (96-KIX) in Henderson-Jackson, TN, Angela Jenkins at KBMS (1480 AM) in Vancouver, WA, and Dr. Alvin Jones of the Paradise Network for having me on your show for almost every book I've written; and to *all* the extraordinary book club members who select my novels for their monthly discussions—thank you, thank you, thank you. And to *all* my readers as a whole—you certainly make all the difference for me as a writer. I am only able to do what I do because of your loyal support, and for that I am forever indebted to all of you.

Much love and God bless you always,

Kimberla Lawson Roby

Email: kim@kimroby.com
Facebook.com/kimberlalawsonroby
Twitter.com/KimberlaLRoby
Instagram.com/kimberlalawsonroby
Periscope.com/kimberlalawsonroby

Reading Group Guide

1. Have you ever known a copycat like Simone? If so, were they copying you or someone else? How did you deal with the situation?

2. What emotions do you feel when you read from Simone's point of view? Can you recognize any of your own thoughts or actions as either similar or even less extreme versions of the way Simone thinks and acts?

3. Simone and Chris have real disagreements about what a marriage should be. For example, they have different views about whether all finances should be joint and whether it is necessary for both partners to belong to the same church. How much give-and-take on issues should there be in a healthy marriage? How do you decide which ones to give in on and which ones to stand fast on?

4. In terms of marital finances, do you believe they should be kept joint or separate? Why or why not?

5. Do you think Chris had a right to go through Simone's things, or should he have respected her privacy even as she lied to him? Was he right to tell Traci about what he discovered? Why or why not?

6. Given the way they treat her and have treated her in the past, do you think Simone still has a responsibility to support her mother and grandmother? Please explain.

7. Simone feels bad when she lies to Traci and is surprised and hurt when Chris leaves her. Do you think she sincerely cares about Traci? About Chris?

8. Simone's identity is tied to her achievements and material possessions. Do you think our culture encourages this sort of thinking more than it used to? Please explain.

9. Traci struggles between her desire to see the best in people and the warnings she gets from family members and her own previous experiences with betrayal. Do you think she was wrong to trust and pity Simone and to want to be her friend? Can she be blamed for her optimistic and forgiving nature? Why or why not?

10. Simone ultimately views herself as a victim. To what extent do you agree with her, if at all? And why do you think she became a copycat to begin with?

11. Simone lacks awareness about how she is copying Traci,

and she does not recognize her own actions in Reverend Black's sermon and Traci's newest book. Is there anything that Chris, Traci, or Robin could have done to help her see what she was doing before it got out of hand? If so, what?

12. At the end of the novel, how do you ultimately feel about Simone? Do you think she will copy her next friend?

35674056811988